THE ROSE OF ASHFORD

RACHEL DOWNING

CORNERSTONETALES.COM

TENDERHEARTED

*T*he sun streamed through the lace curtains of Roseworth Cottage, painting the dining room in warm honey tones. Holly Clarke sat at the worn wooden table, its surface cluttered with crumbs from breakfast rolls and a half-empty pot of blackberry jam. She traced patterns in the scattered flour dust whilst the gentle chorus of finches drifted through the open window.

Holly dabbed at her mouth with the napkin—one of Mother's finest pieces, embroidered with tiny rosebuds along the edges. The delicate thread work caught the morning light as she folded it carefully beside her plate.

In the kitchen, her mother moved with practised grace, the copper kettle singing on the hob. Mary Clarke hummed softly, a hymn Holly recognised from last Sunday's service. Her mother's slender fingers arranged fresh-cut roses in the blue china vase, their petals still jewelled with morning dew.

"These beauties opened just this morning." Her mother tucked a wayward stem into place. "The pink ones always bloom first, eager little things."

The sweet perfume of roses mingled with the earthy scent of

breakfast tea, creating that particular fragrance Holly associated with home—with safety and love and everything right in the world.

The door creaked, and Reverend Thomas Clarke entered, his black clerical coat rustling against the doorframe. Morning light caught the silver threads beginning to show in his dark hair. He crossed the room in three long strides and knelt beside Holly's chair, his broad hand gentle as he ruffled her auburn locks.

"And how's my little sparrow this morning?"

Holly giggled at the familiar nickname. "Papa, sparrows are brown. My hair's like Mother's."

"Indeed it is." Her father pulled his leather Bible from his coat pocket, the pages worn soft from years of use. "But sparrows are also clever and kind, sharing their nests with others who need shelter."

He took Holly's small hands in his weathered ones, his wedding band glinting as he opened to a marked passage. "Listen carefully, my dear. 'Be ye kind one to another, tender-hearted, forgiving one another.'"

Holly's fingers curled around his thumb, feeling the calluses from his garden work.

"Do you understand what that means?"

"To share?" Holly ventured. "Like when I gave my biscuit to Timothy yesterday because he forgot his lunch?"

"Precisely." Her father's brown eyes crinkled at the corners. "God smiles when we open our hearts to others."

He gestured around the cottage, encompassing the comfortable sitting room visible through the doorway, the paintings on the walls, the roses nodding at the windows.

"This cottage itself is a reminder of God's providence. Your mother's grandmother left it to us—an inheritance that became our sanctuary." His voice carried that particular reverence he reserved for blessings. "Not everyone receives such gifts, Holly.

Your grandmama could have left it to anyone, but God guided her heart to provide for your mother."

Her mother approached, setting down the teapot with a soft clink. "Your father's right, darling. We're blessed beyond measure."

Her father stood, his knees creaking slightly. "Which is why we must always remember those less fortunate. This cottage, these roses, even our morning bread—they're not ours alone. They're tools for God's work."

Holly nodded solemnly, though she didn't fully grasp the weight of his words. She simply knew that her father helped everyone—from Mrs Bates with her painful joints to the travelling families who sometimes camped near the church.

"Now then," Her father said, straightening his coat, "I must prepare for Mrs Whitworth's visit. She's bringing her nephew—poor lad's just lost his position at the mill."

As he departed, Holly watched the sun climb higher, transforming the cottage's stone walls to gold.

MORNING LESSONS

*H*olly's mother cleared the breakfast table with practised efficiency, stacking plates whilst Holly gathered the last crumbs into her palm for the robins outside. Her mother disappeared into the parlour and returned with an armful of books, their spines faded from years of handling.

"Time for your lessons, my darling." She set them down with care, adding Holly's embroidery basket beside them. "Which shall we begin with today?"

Holly reached immediately for the book on top—a collection of moral tales bound in green cloth, its corners worn soft. The pages fell open to a familiar spot, and there, in her mother's careful script along the margins, were notes: *Remember to pause here* and *Holly struggled with this word —practise.*

Her finger traced the elegant loops of her mother's handwriting. Each annotation marked a moment they'd shared, bent over these very pages whilst rain pattered against the windows or summer breezes stirred the curtains.

"Shall I read 'The Good Samaritan'?" Holly settled into her chair, back straight as Mother had taught her.

"Please do." Mary picked up her own needlework, though her eyes remained on her daughter.

Holly began, her voice clear and measured. She navigated the difficult passages without stumbling, pronouncing each word with careful precision. When she reached the part about binding wounds, she remembered to pause—just as the margin note suggested—letting the weight of mercy settle in the air.

"Oh, Holly." Her mother's needle stilled mid-stitch. "Your reading has improved remarkably. You didn't hesitate once at 'Jericho' this time."

Pride bloomed warm in Holly's chest. She closed the book gently, treating it with the reverence her mother had taught her. Books were treasures, windows to worlds beyond Roseworth's gardens.

"Might we have music before we continue?" Holly stood, already moving toward the sitting room. "I've been practising the piece you showed me."

They crossed through the doorway where morning light streamed across the old Turkish carpet. The pianoforte stood against the far wall, its walnut case gleaming despite the small scratches that marked its age. It had belonged to Mother's family for generations, another inheritance that had found its way to their cottage.

Holly lifted the lid, revealing keys yellowed like old teeth but still true in tone. She positioned her hands as Mother had shown her—wrists level, fingers curved as though holding small plums. The bench creaked as she adjusted her position.

The first notes rang out, bright and certain. Holly's fingers found their rhythm, dancing across the keys in a country dance her mother had taught her last month. Her tongue poked slightly between her lips as she concentrated on a particularly tricky passage, where the left hand had to leap whilst the right maintained its melody.

Sunlight caught the dust motes spinning above the

pianoforte, turning them to tiny golden coins. Holly's auburn hair fell forward as she leant into the more vigorous section, her small body swaying with the music's momentum. She missed a note—her ring finger landing on F instead of F sharp—but continued without pause, just as Mother always instructed.

The final chord resonated through the cottage. Holly held her position for a moment, hands poised above the keys, before turning to gauge her mother's reaction.

Her mother stood in the doorway, her eyes bright with something that looked almost like tears. "That was beautiful, my little gift. Your father will want to hear it when he returns."

Holly beamed, her fingers already itching to begin again, to perfect that troublesome passage. The morning stretched ahead, full of words to read and music to master, each lesson another stitch in the tapestry her parents wove around her with such tender care.

ROSES

*H*olly burst through the cottage door, her lesson books abandoned on the table behind her. The late morning air carried the perfume of roses—sweet and heady, drawing her into the garden like a moth to flame. Her boots scattered gravel as she ran, skirt catching on the lavender that bordered the path.

The rose garden sprawled before her, a riot of colour against the cottage's weathered stone. Pink climbers scaled the walls whilst white tea roses clustered near the garden bench. Each bloom nodded in the gentle breeze, as though greeting her arrival. Holly slowed her pace, breathing deeply. This was her mother's domain, cultivated with the same patience she brought to Holly's lessons.

"Careful with your dress," Her mother called, emerging from the cottage with her gardening basket. She'd changed into an older frock, one already bearing the battle scars of thorns and soil.

Holly was already kneeling beside a particularly vigorous damask rose, its branches sprawling beyond their allotted space. "This one's grown wild, Mother."

"Sometimes they need a firm hand." Her mother knelt beside her, producing a pair of worn secateurs. "Watch closely. We cut just above the leaf node, at an angle. Like this."

The blade sliced clean through the woody stem. Holly took the secateurs when offered, their weight substantial in her small hands. She selected a branch, positioning the blades as shown. The cut wasn't as clean as her mother's, but the branch fell away neatly.

"Well done." Mary guided Holly's hands to the next cut. "My grandmother taught me this when I was your age. She'd say the roses were like people—they needed both tenderness and discipline to truly flourish."

Holly's fingers worked alongside her mother's, pulling away dead blooms and wayward branches. Soil crept beneath her nails, leaving dark crescents she'd have to scrub later. A thorn caught her thumb, drawing a bead of blood she quickly pressed against her apron.

"Your grandmother's roses?" Holly touched a particularly beautiful bloom, its petals the colour of fresh cream.

"These very ones. She planted them the year she married. Through harsh winters and dry summers, they endured." Mary sat back on her heels, surveying their work. "When times were difficult—when we had little money or faced hardship—she'd bring me here. 'Look at the roses, Mary,' she'd say. 'They bloom again every year, no matter how hard the pruning.'"

Holly studied her mother's face, seeing the faraway look that meant she was travelling back through memory. The sun caught the auburn in Mary's hair—the same shade as Holly's own—making it glow like burnished copper.

"Is that why you tend them so carefully?"

"Partly." Mary cupped a bloom in her palm, inhaling its fragrance. "But also because beauty requires effort. Nothing worthwhile comes without work, my darling. Remember that."

They worked until the sun climbed higher, filling two

baskets with cuttings for the compost heap. Holly's hands were properly filthy now, her pinafore bearing streaks of green from the stems. Mother didn't scold—she simply smiled and suggested Holly wash before joining the village children.

Holly scrubbed her hands in the kitchen basin. Through the window, she could hear voices from the common field beyond their gate. She dried her hands hastily on her apron and darted outside.

"Holly!" young Tom Miller waved from across the field. "We're playing knights and dragons!"

She ran to join them, her morning of quiet lessons forgotten in the rush of childhood games. They fashioned swords from fallen branches and shields from barrel lids someone had salvaged. Holly became a brave knight, then a fearsome dragon, then a princess who rescued herself—much to the boys' confusion.

As she chased little Sarah Henshaw across the grass, Holly's mind wandered to the stories her father read after evening prayers. Tales of faraway lands where mountains touched the sky and oceans stretched beyond the horizon. What would it be like to sail those seas? To climb those peaks?

"You're not catching me proper!" Sarah complained, pulling Holly from her reverie.

But even as Holly renewed her pursuit, laughing as Sarah squealed and dodged, part of her remained in those imagined places. She thought of the maps in Father's study, the ones with blank spaces marked 'unknown.' Someday, perhaps, she might fill in those spaces herself. She'd return to tell Mother and Father of her adventures, bringing back roses from distant gardens to plant alongside Grandmother's.

The afternoon sun warmed her face as she ran, her spirit soaring with possibility.

SUNDAY DEVOTIONS

The church bells rang out across Ashford Green, their bronze voices calling the faithful to worship. Holly's Sunday shoes clicked against the cobblestones as she walked between her parents, her small hand enclosed in her mother's gentle grip. The familiar weight of her prayer book pressed against her side, tucked beneath her arm.

Other families emerged from their cottages, converging on the old stone church at the village centre. Mrs Whitfield nodded to them, her three boys trailing behind like ducklings. Old Mr Garrett tipped his cap to Holly's father, who returned the gesture with warmth.

"Mind the puddle," her mother guided Holly around a patch of muddy water left from yesterday's rain. The autumn air carried woodsmoke and the faint sweetness of apples from someone's orchard.

St Nicholas's stood before them, its weathered stones speaking of centuries of worship. Holly traced the worn grooves in the doorway where countless hands had steadied themselves whilst entering. Inside, the air hung thick with beeswax and that particular mustiness that belonged to ancient buildings.

Their pew sat third from the front—close enough to hear every word clearly, but not so prominent as to appear presumptuous. Holly slid along the polished wood, arranging her skirt properly as Mother had taught her. The congregation settled around them in rustling waves of fabric and whispered greetings.

When Father ascended to the pulpit, transformation overtook him. The man who read her bedtime stories became something larger, his voice filling the vaulted space without strain. Holly watched his warm brown eyes move across the gathered faces—lingering on widow Bates in her threadbare shawl, pausing at the Jennings family with their new baby, acknowledging young Peter Cromwell who'd just returned from failed prospects in the city.

"We gather today to speak of providence," her father began, his hands resting lightly on the worn Bible before him. "Not the providence of grand gestures, but the quiet miracles found in daily bread shared with neighbours."

Holly recognised the cadence of his speech—the way he built his thoughts like her mother built garden walls, each stone carefully placed to support the next. He spoke of the loaves and fishes, but somehow made it about Mrs Henderson sharing her preserves with the Turner family after their father took ill.

The sermon wove through scripture and village life until they became inseparable. Holly found herself leaning forward, though she'd heard variations of these themes countless times at their breakfast table. Here, amongst the community, the words took on different weight.

When the collection plate passed, Holly watched her father's eyes follow its progress. He knew precisely who gave what they could spare and who gave beyond their means. His expression never changed, but she recognised the tiny crease between his brows that meant he was already planning tomorrow's visits.

After the final hymn, the congregation spilled into the churchyard. Holly stood beside her parents as villagers approached with their concerns and their gratitude. Thomas Hartley mentioned his wife's continued illness. The Coopers shared news of their son's apprenticeship. Each exchange added another strand to the web of connection Father maintained.

"Reverend Clarke," Mrs Whitworth approached, the nephew she'd mentioned yesterday hovering behind her shoulder. The boy looked gaunt, his clothes hanging loose on his frame. "This is James."

Father extended his hand to the boy, who took it hesitantly. "Welcome to Ashford Green, James. Mrs Whitworth tells me you're skilled with numbers. Mr Jones at the counting house might have need of such talents."

Hope flickered across the boy's face. Holly watched this small resurrection—how a few words from Father could restore what hardship had stolen.

As they walked home, Mother's hand found Holly's again. The afternoon stretched before them, and Holly knew what came next. Already, she could see Father mentally cataloguing what remained in their pantry, calculating how many parcels they could prepare.

"Will we visit Mrs Bates today?" Holly asked, though she suspected the answer.

"After we prepare the baskets," her father confirmed, his stride purposeful but unhurried. "She mentioned her roof leaked during the last rain. I'll need to speak with Mr Harrison about repairs."

The cottage appeared around the bend, roses still blooming despite the lateness of the season. Holly thought of her great grandmother's words about resilience, about beauty requiring effort. Perhaps charity was like gardening—constant work that bloomed in ways you couldn't always see.

Their Sunday had only just begun.

SIMPLE BLESSINGS

*R*ain drummed against the cottage windows in steady rhythm, transforming the afternoon into a cocoon of warmth and gentle activity. Holly sat cross-legged on the hearth rug, her embroidery hoop balanced carefully in her lap whilst Mother arranged dried lavender and rosemary along the mantelpiece. The kitchen beckoned with the golden scent of honey cakes cooling on the sill.

"Mind your tension," her mother murmured, settling beside Holly with her own needlework. "Too tight and the fabric puckers. Too loose and your stitches won't hold."

Holly examined her work—a simple daisy taking shape on the corner of what would become Father's Christmas handkerchief. The white petals emerged slowly under her needle, each stitch requiring concentration that made her tongue peek between her lips.

"Why daisies, Mother?" Holly adjusted her grip on the needle, trying to match the even spacing Mother achieved so effortlessly.

"Your grandmother always said daisies meant new beginnings." Her mother's own needle moved in fluid motions, creating intricate rosebuds that seemed to bloom beneath her fingers. "She embroidered them on everything when she first came to Roseworth as a bride—pillowcases, tablecloths, even Father's Sunday waistcoat."

Holly paused mid-stitch. "Will you teach me roses next?"

"When your daisies can stand without wobbling." Her mother's gentle laugh took any sting from the words. "Each flower has its season, little sparrow. Daisies teach patience. Roses teach precision. Forget-me-nots teach delicacy."

The fire crackled, sending shadows dancing across their work. Holly lost herself in the rhythm—pierce, pull, pierce, pull—whilst Mother's voice wove stories around each bloom. Violets for modesty, ivy for fidelity, lilacs for first love. The handkerchief became a garden of meanings, each tiny stitch carrying generations of feminine wisdom.

When the rain finally ceased, her father appeared in the doorway, shaking droplets from his coat. "The sun's breaking through. Shall we venture out before it disappears again?"

Holly set aside her embroidery with relief. Her fingers ached from the close work, and the promise of fresh air called to her restless spirit. She fetched her cloak whilst her father waited by the door, his eyes already distant with that particular expression that meant he was cataloguing God's handiwork.

The countryside glistened like a newly polished mirror. Puddles reflected clouds racing overhead, and every blade of grass wore diamonds of moisture. Holly's boots squished through the muddy lane as they headed toward the meadow beyond the cottage garden.

"Look there," her father pointed to a cluster of late-blooming elderflowers drooping heavy with rain. "See how they bend but don't break? That's wisdom worth remembering."

Holly gathered her skirt to crouch beside a patch of wild mint, breathing deeply of its sharp sweetness. "Why does everything smell stronger after rain?"

"The earth releases what it's been holding." Her father knelt beside her, his large hands gentle as he showed her how to identify the serrated leaves. "Rain washes away the dust, lets the true scents emerge. Rather like prayer, wouldn't you say?"

They walked deeper into the meadow, her father's knowledge transforming every step into discovery. He showed her how to distinguish between edible and poisonous berries, how to read the weather in cloud formations, how the direction of moss growth revealed true north. Holly filled her apron pockets with interesting stones and late wildflowers, already imagining where she might plant similar varieties in next year's garden.

"Father," she said, clutching a bunch of purple clover, "when I'm grown, I want a garden ten times larger than ours."

"Do you indeed?" His warm eyes crinkled with amusement. "And who will tend this magnificent garden?"

"I will. Every morning before breakfast, every evening after supper." Holly's voice grew more animated as the vision expanded. "I'll have roses and lavender and herbs for cooking, and a special section just for wildflowers where children can come and pick bouquets for their mothers."

Her father paused beside a weathered stile, studying her earnest face. "That's a beautiful dream, little sparrow. But remember—the gardener who tends ten plots poorly serves no one. Better to nurture one small patch with all your heart than spread yourself thin across vast holdings."

Holly considered this as they turned homeward. The cottage appeared around the bend, smoke curling from its chimney like an invitation. Perhaps Father was right. Perhaps the dream wasn't about size but about care.

Evening found them gathered in the sitting room, the fire rebuilt to chase away autumn's encroaching chill. Father settled into his favourite chair with the family Bible whilst Holly and Mother arranged themselves on the settee, embroidery set aside for tomorrow's lesson.

"Tonight we'll read of the talents," her father announced, opening to a well-worn page. His voice filled the room as he read of servants entrusted with their master's treasure—some who invested wisely, others who buried their gifts in fear.

"What does it mean, Father?" Holly leaned forward, her green eyes reflecting firelight. "About hiding talents in the ground?"

Her mother smoothed Holly's auburn hair. "It means God gives each of us gifts—like your way with plants, or your musical ear. The question becomes what we do with those gifts."

"But what if we're not certain what our talents are?" Holly's brow furrowed with the weight of ten-year-old philosophy.

Her father closed the Bible, keeping his finger marking the page. "That's why we have time to discover them, little sparrow. Your talents will reveal themselves through what brings you joy and serves others well. The gardener in you, the musician, the tender heart that notices when Mrs Bates needs wood for her fire—these are all talents worth cultivating."

The evening wound down in comfortable silence, the three of them bound together by shared stories and gentle teaching. Outside, night settled over Ashford Green like a familiar blanket. Tomorrow would bring new lessons, new discoveries, new opportunities to tend the gifts they'd been given.

Holly drifted toward sleep thinking of daisies and talents, of gardens yet to be planted and songs yet to be learned. In the safety of Roseworth Cottage, surrounded by love and wisdom, the future seemed as limitless as the wildflower meadows beyond their door.

VILLAGE BONDS

$\mathcal{T}$he morning of the autumn fair dawned crisp and bright, painting Ashford Green in shades of gold and amber. Holly pressed her face against the cottage window, watching villagers erect stalls and string bunting between the ancient oaks. The entire village hummed with preparation—children darted between adults' legs whilst mothers called after them, and the sweet aroma of fresh-baked pies drifted on the breeze.

"Come away from there, little sparrow," her father chuckled, entering with his arms full of firewood. "You'll fog the glass with all that eager breathing."

Holly spun round, her green eyes sparkling. "May we go soon? Mrs Henshaw said there would be puppet shows and dancing, and Tom Miller promised to show me how to win at the ring toss."

"First we must prepare our contribution." Her mother emerged from the kitchen, wiping flour from her hands. "The roses won't arrange themselves."

Holly's heart leapt. For weeks, they'd planned their booth for the fair—a display of Roseworth's finest blooms paired with

Mother's seedcakes and Father's carved wooden crosses. Holly had been granted the honour of selecting which roses to cut, a responsibility that made her feel quite grown-up indeed.

In the garden, morning dew still clung to the petals like scattered pearls. Holly moved carefully between the bushes, basket in hand, choosing only the most perfect specimens. A deep crimson damask here, pale pink gallicas there, and her favourite —the white alba roses that climbed the cottage wall like faithful sentinels.

"Mind the thorns," Her mother cautioned, following with sharp garden shears. "Beauty often comes armed for protection."

Holly nodded solemnly, though she'd already learnt that lesson through numerous tiny pricks. Each rose required careful handling, respect for its defences. She watched Mother's practised hands work, noting how she cut the stems at an angle beneath running water, how she stripped away lower leaves that might spoil in the vase.

"There," her mother stepped back, surveying their morning's work. "Fit for the Queen herself, wouldn't you say?"

The fair transformed the village green into a wonderland of colour and sound. Holly clutched her father's hand as they navigated between stalls selling everything from ribbons to roasted chestnuts. A fiddler played beneath the elm tree whilst children danced in circles, their laughter rising above the general din.

"Holly! Holly, over here!" Sarah Henshaw waved frantically from beside the coconut, her brown plaits bouncing with excitement. Tom Miller stood nearby, his freckled face split by an enormous grin.

"Go on then," her father squeezed her hand gently. "We'll be at our booth when you're ready."

Holly scampered toward her friends, her heart singing with pure joy. Sarah grabbed her arm immediately, tugging her toward a cluster of older children gathered near the Morris dancers.

"Look what Jane Porter's brought!" Sarah whispered conspir-atorially, gesturing toward a girl of perhaps twelve who held a wooden box filled with what appeared to be tiny kittens.

Holly gasped with delight. The kittens mewed softly, their eyes barely open, their fur like silk against her fingertips when Jane allowed her to stroke one. The little creatures reminded her of the roses in Mother's garden—delicate, requiring gentle care, beautiful beyond measure.

"Their mother disappeared," Jane explained sadly. "Father says we can't keep them all, but I can't bear to see them go hungry."

Without hesitation, Holly reached into her pocket, with-drawing the penny Father had given her for fairground treats. "For milk," she said simply, pressing the coin into Jane's palm. "Growing things need proper nourishment."

Tom Miller's eyes widened with admiration. "That was your sweet money, Holly Clarke."

Holly shrugged, though warmth spread through her chest at the grateful tears in Jane's eyes. "Mother always says kindness costs nothing but pays the richest dividends."

The afternoon flew by in a whirlwind of games and laughter. Holly tried her hand at the ring toss under Tom's patient instruction, sampled Mrs Baker's famous toffee apples, and joined the younger children in a rousing game of blind man's bluff. When the church bells chimed four o'clock, she realised she'd barely visited her parents' booth.

She found them surrounded by admirers, Mother explaining the different rose varieties whilst Father demonstrated his woodcarving technique. Their display had drawn quite a crowd —the roses' fragrance and Mother's warm manner proving irre-sistible to passing villagers.

"There's our little gardener," her father announced as Holly approached, slipping his arm around her shoulders. "How fares the fair, sparrow?"

"Wonderful!" Holly beamed up at him, then turned to address the gathered crowd. "These roses came from my grandmother's bushes. Mother taught me how to choose the best ones, and how to cut them so they'll last longest in water."

An elderly woman nodded approvingly. "Wise lessons for one so young. Gardens teach patience better than any schoolmaster."

As evening approached and the fair began winding down, Holly found herself seated on a hay bale with Sarah and Tom, sharing the last of Mother's seedcakes. The fiddler had switched to gentler melodies, and families gathered their tired children for the walk home.

"This was the best day," Sarah sighed contentedly, crumbs dotting her apron.

Holly nodded, watching her parents pack away their remaining roses with the same care they'd shown arranging them. The whole day felt like a gift—the sunshine, the laughter, the warmth of community that wrapped around them all like one of Mother's quilts. Even Jane's kittens had found homes, adopted by families charmed by their tiny mews and soft fur.

Walking home through the gathering dusk, Holly's hand secure in her mother's while her father carried the empty basket, she felt rich beyond measure. The cottage windows glowed welcomingly ahead, promising supper and stories by the fire. Tomorrow would bring ordinary lessons and chores, but tonight belonged to memory—to laughter shared and kindness given, to the sweet knowledge that she belonged to this place and these people who loved her.

DANIEL THORNHILL

*D*aniel Thornhill sat at the grand oak table in his father's study, surrounded by leather-bound volumes that seemed to watch him with silent authority. The afternoon sun streamed through tall windows, casting golden rectangles across the polished wood where treatises on common law and judicial procedure lay open before him. At twelve years old, the weight of expectation pressed upon his shoulders like an invisible cloak—one day, these books would guide his profession, these principles would shape his decisions.

He traced his finger along a passage about magistrates' duties, the words swimming slightly as his mind wandered. Father spoke often of justice, of serving the community through law, of the Thornhill family's long tradition of public service. Daniel understood the honour in such work, yet sometimes he wondered if he possessed the natural authority his father wielded so effortlessly.

"Daniel?" Sir Richard's voice carried from the doorway. "Ready for our visit to the parsonage?"

Daniel closed the volume carefully, rising from his chair

with the practiced composure his tutors had instilled. "Yes, Father."

The leather satchel by his chair contained simple gifts—peppermint sweets from London, a collection of moral tales suitable for a young reader, and a small wooden toy horse his father had suggested might delight the Clarke child. Daniel had chosen each item thoughtfully, though he couldn't quite articulate why such gestures mattered so deeply to him.

The carriage ride to Ashford Green proved pleasant, and the short walk from the stables to Roseworth cottage even more so, with the autumn air crisp against his face. His father spoke of parish matters and Reverend Clarke's admirable work among the poor, but Daniel found himself studying the countryside with fresh eyes. Thornhill Manor, grand though it was, sometimes felt cold despite its luxury—all marble and mahogany, designed to impress rather than comfort.

Roseworth Cottage appeared ahead like something from a storybook. Roses climbed the stone walls in magnificent profusion, their blooms creating a tapestry of pink and white against weathered grey. The very air seemed warmer here, scented with flowers and something indefinably welcoming that made Daniel's chest tighten with unexpected longing.

"Beautiful gardens," his father observed approvingly. "Mrs Clarke tends them herself, I'm told. Remarkable dedication."

Daniel nodded, though movement near the cottage wall caught his eye. A young girl, perhaps ten years old, sat cross-legged on the grass with a bowl of milk beside her. Three scrawny cats approached cautiously, their ribs visible beneath patchy fur. The girl—this must be Holly Clarke—spoke softly to them, her voice carrying notes of encouragement and comfort.

"Come on then," she whispered to a particularly timid tabby. "There's plenty for everyone."

Daniel found himself studying her face as she divided the milk carefully between shallow dishes, ensuring each cat received equal portions. Auburn hair caught the sunlight, and when she turned slightly, he glimpsed bright green eyes filled with gentle determination. Something about her earnestness stirred unfamiliar feelings in his chest—admiration, certainly, but also curiosity about the kind of person who would sacrifice her own comfort for hungry strays.

The cottage door opened before they could knock, and Reverend Clarke emerged with arms spread wide in welcome. His face bore the same gentle warmth Daniel remembered from church services, though up close the man seemed younger than his pulpit presence suggested.

"Sir Richard! Master Daniel!" The reverend's handshake proved firm yet kind. "What a pleasure to have you visit our humble home. Mary will be delighted—she's just finishing her roses."

Daniel followed his father through a doorway that required the magistrate to duck slightly. Inside, the cottage embraced them with warmth that had nothing to do with the fire crackling in the hearth. Dried herbs hung from ceiling beams, their scent mingling with fresh bread and something floral that spoke of careful housekeeping and loving attention.

The kitchen bustled with quiet activity. Mrs Clarke turned from the hob where a kettle whistled softly, her face brightening at their arrival. Flour dusted her apron, and wisps of auburn hair escaped her cap, giving her an approachable beauty that put Daniel instantly at ease.

"Sir Richard, Master Daniel, welcome to Roseworth." Her curtsy carried genuine pleasure rather than mere politeness. "Holly, come say hello to our visitors."

The girl from the garden appeared in the doorway, no longer kneeling among cats but standing with careful posture that spoke of recent instruction in proper manners. Her green eyes studied Daniel with frank curiosity, and he found himself straightening under her gaze.

"Holly, this is Master Daniel Thornhill," her father said gently. "His father serves as magistrate in Ashford."

Holly executed a perfect curtsy, though Daniel caught the slight wobble that suggested recent practice. "Pleased to meet you, Master Daniel."

"Miss Clarke." His own bow felt stiff compared to her natural grace. "Your garden is beautiful."

"Mother tends the roses, but I help with weeding." Pride coloured her voice. "Would you like to see the climbing rose? It's nearly as tall as the cottage roof."

The adults settled into conversation about parish matters and village concerns, their voices creating a comfortable background hum. Reverend Clarke gestured toward the garden with an indulgent smile.

"Why don't you children explore outside? The afternoon's fine, and Holly knows every interesting corner of our grounds."

Daniel glanced at his father, who nodded approvingly. Sir Richard valued social connections, particularly those that demonstrated the family's commitment to community relationships.

Outside, Holly transformed from the careful girl of the kitchen into something wilder and more vibrant. She pointed out flower varieties with enthusiastic detail, showed him where field mice nested under the garden wall, and explained her system for caring for the stray cats.

"That's Duchess," she said, indicating a grey tabby sunning herself on a garden stone. "She's expecting kittens soon. And the orange one is Biscuit—he only has three legs, but he catches more mice than any cat in the village."

Daniel found her knowledge impressive. At Thornhill Manor, cats existed primarily to control vermin, and he'd never considered their individual personalities or circumstances.

"There's an old apple tree past the rose hedge," Holly continued, already heading toward a gap in the flowering bushes. "The best climbing tree in all of Ashford Green."

The ancient apple tree stood gnarled and inviting, its lowest branches within easy reach. Holly gathered her skirt with practiced efficiency and pulled herself up with confidence that spoke of frequent climbing adventures.

"Come on," she called down to him. "You can see the whole village from the top branches."

Daniel hesitated. His tutors had never included tree climbing in their curriculum, and his good clothes seemed inappropriate for such activity. But Holly's expectant face and the challenge in her bright eyes stirred something adventurous in his chest.

He grasped the lowest branch and hauled himself up, surprised by his own capability. Holly had already reached a comfortable perch several feet above, her legs swinging freely as she waited for him to catch up.

"Mind that branch there—it's not as strong as it looks." She pointed to a suspicious-looking limb. "I learned that lesson the hard way."

Daniel climbed carefully, matching her route through the branches. The view from Holly's chosen spot proved worth the effort—the cottage nestled below them like a perfect miniature, surrounded by rose gardens that seemed even more magnificent from above.

"It's wonderful," he said softly, meaning more than just the view.

Holly beamed at his approval, then shifted position to point toward the village. The movement proved too ambitious. Her foot slipped on the smooth bark, and she tumbled down two branches before catching herself against the trunk.

"Ow!" She pressed her hand to her knee where a scraped patch showed bright against her torn stocking.

Daniel scrambled down immediately, his heart racing with concern. "Are you hurt badly?"

Holly examined the scrape with matter-of-fact assessment. "It's not deep. I've had worse from helping Papa fix the chicken coop."

But Daniel noticed her wince as she bent her leg, saw the way she bit her lip against the sting. Without thinking, he reached into his satchel and produced his neatly folded handkerchief—crisp white linen with his initials embroidered in blue silk thread.

"Here, you can use this." The words emerged softer than intended, his cheeks warming with sudden shyness. The handkerchief represented his most prized possession, a gift from his mother for his twelfth birthday, yet offering it felt completely natural.

Holly's eyes widened with surprise. "But it's so fine—I'll get blood on it."

"That's what handkerchiefs are for." He pressed it gently into her hands, their fingers brushing briefly. "To help when someone's hurt."

She dabbed carefully at the scrape, her movements reverent as though handling something precious. When she looked up, her green eyes sparkled with genuine gratitude.

"Thank you, Daniel. That's very kind."

The warmth in her voice and the use of his Christian name sent unexpected pleasure through his chest. For this moment, the difference between magistrate's son and clergyman's daughter disappeared entirely, leaving only two children sharing simple kindness in an apple tree.

The carriage wheels rolled steadily along the country lane, carrying Daniel and his father back toward Thornhill Manor as afternoon shadows lengthened across the fields. Daniel sat quietly beside Sir Richard, his satchel resting on his lap, but his thoughts refused to settle on the passing countryside.

Instead, his mind kept returning to Roseworth Cottage—to Holly's bright laughter echoing from the apple tree, the careful way she'd tended to each stray cat, and how her auburn hair had caught the late sunlight like burnished copper. The memory of her genuine gratitude when he'd offered his handkerchief stirred something warm in his chest that he couldn't quite name.

He'd encountered many young ladies at social gatherings with his parents, daughters of fellow magistrates and barristers who spoke in measured tones about appropriate subjects. Yet none had possessed Holly's natural ease or the spark of genuine kindness that seemed to illuminate her every gesture. When she'd explained her system for caring for wounded animals or pointed out which flowers needed extra water, she'd spoken with purpose that went beyond mere politeness.

Daniel found himself puzzling over what it meant to be truly kind-hearted in a world that often prioritised duty and social standing above compassion. Holly seemed to navigate both effortlessly—showing proper respect to her parents whilst also climbing trees and rescuing stray cats without a moment's hesitation.

"The Clarkes are exemplary parishioners," His father remarked, breaking into Daniel's contemplations. "Reverend Clarke's dedication to his congregation sets a standard few clergymen achieve."

"Yes, Father." Daniel straightened, grateful for the opening. "They seem genuinely devoted to helping others."

That evening at dinner, his father continued discussing their charitable visits whilst carving the roasted fowl. The dining room's mahogany table gleamed under candlelight, reflecting the polished silver and fine china that marked their comfortable circumstances.

"Compassion without action remains merely sentiment," his father explained, serving Daniel a generous portion. "Those blessed with means bear responsibility to assist the less fortunate. It's not charity—it's duty."

Daniel nodded, absorbing his father's words with newfound attention. These principles had always formed part of his education, discussed in abstract terms during lessons about justice and social responsibility. But Holly's example had given them tangible meaning. She possessed little material wealth yet gave freely from what she had—sharing her penny for milk, offering shelter to wounded creatures, treating each person with genuine warmth.

"How does one balance helping others with social expectations?" Daniel asked carefully.

His father paused, studying his son with interest. "An excellent question. True nobility lies not in title or wealth, but in character. Those who use their advantages to lift others demonstrate the finest qualities of their breeding."

After dinner, Daniel settled in the library with his law books, intending to review the day's studies. His father had always pushed him to excel beyond his years. Whilst other twelve-year-olds played with hoops and marbles, Daniel grappled with Blackstone's Commentaries and studied property law. "Early preparation ensures future success," his father frequently reminded him. "When you reach Cambridge, you'll possess advantages your peers lack."

Daniel appreciated the privilege of advanced education, yet tonight he wondered what other experiences he might be missing.

The fireplace crackled warmly, casting dancing shadows across the leather-bound volumes that lined the walls. But concentration proved impossible as his thoughts kept drifting back to Holly's animated explanations about her garden and her matter-of-fact acceptance of his help.

He closed his book with a soft thud, staring into the flickering flames. How could he emulate Holly's natural kindness? Surely opportunities would present themselves. Daniel resolved to always keep alert and on the look-out for such occasions.

The firelight illuminated his thoughtful expression as determination took root in his chest. Holly had shown him that true courage lay not in grand gestures but in everyday kindnesses—feeding hungry cats, sharing precious resources, treating everyone with equal dignity regardless of their station.

Later, as Daniel prepared for sleep in his comfortable chamber, anticipation stirred within him. Perhaps his father would make another visit to Roseworth Cottage soon. The thought of seeing Holly again, of learning more from her bright spirit and genuine nature, filled him with hope.

He imagined future conversations where he might demonstrate his own growth in kindness, where their friendship could deepen beyond a single afternoon's encounter. As sleep approached, Daniel resolved to carry Holly's example with him —a reminder that nobility of character mattered far more than nobility of birth.

CHRISTMAS EVE

*H*olly sat beside her mother in the familiar wooden pew, the polished surface smooth beneath her hands as she gazed around St Nicholas Church in wonder. Tonight felt different from their usual Sunday services—the ancient stone walls seemed to glow with warmth, draped in garlands of fresh pine that filled the air with their crisp, sweet fragrance. Fat candles flickered from every available surface, their golden light dancing across the faces of neighbours and friends who had gathered for Christmas Eve service.

The scent of mulled wine drifted from the vestry where Mrs Henshaw and the other ladies had prepared refreshments for after the service. Holly breathed deeply, catching hints of cinnamon and cloves that made her stomach flutter with anticipation. Christmas Eve had always been her favourite service of the year—when the whole village came together to celebrate the birth of Christ, when even the most reluctant churchgoers found their way to the pews.

Children whispered excitedly throughout the congregation, their voices creating a gentle hum beneath the organ's prelude. Young Timothy Evans kept craning his neck to peer at the candles on the altar, whilst his sister clutched a small wooden angel that their father had carved especially for the occasion. Holly smiled at their obvious excitement, remembering how magical Christmas Eve had seemed when she was even smaller.

Her gaze swept across the filled pews until it landed on a familiar figure several rows ahead. Daniel Thornhill sat between his parents, his dark hair neatly combed and his posture straight as he listened attentively to the service. Holly's heart gave a small leap of delight—she hadn't expected to see him here tonight. The Thornhills usually attended the larger church in the city of Ashford, but perhaps they had chosen St Nicholas for the special intimacy of Christmas Eve.

"Look, Mother," Holly whispered, tugging gently on Mary's sleeve. "The Thornhills are here."

Mary followed her daughter's gaze and smiled warmly. "How lovely. We must be sure to greet them after service."

Holly nodded eagerly, already imagining showing Daniel the new roses that had begun to bloom in their winter garden.

The organ's notes swelled as her father appeared at the front of the church, his familiar figure commanding yet gentle as he approached the pulpit. Holly felt that familiar surge of pride watching him—the way the congregation's attention focused entirely on him, the respect evident in every upturned face. Tonight he wore his finest vestments, the deep purple stole draped across his shoulders catching the candlelight.

"My dear friends," Reverend Clarke's voice resonated through the stone sanctuary, warm and clear as it reached every corner. "On this most blessed of nights, we gather to celebrate the greatest gift ever bestowed upon mankind—the birth of our Lord and Saviour, Jesus Christ."

Holly leaned forward slightly, captivated by her father's words. She had heard him preach countless times, but something about Christmas Eve always made his sermons feel more magical, more alive with possibility.

"In the darkest season of the year," he continued, his eyes moving across the congregation, "when the nights are longest and the cold most bitter, we are reminded that hope can bloom even in the bleakest circumstances. Just as Mary carried the Christ child in her womb through the uncertainty of travel and the harshness of winter, so too must we carry hope in our hearts through whatever trials may come."

The congregation listened in rapt attention, children temporarily forgetting their excitement as his words painted pictures of that first Christmas night. Holly noticed how Mrs Bates, seated in her usual back pew, leaned forward to catch every word despite her failing hearing.

Around them, voices joined in the familiar Christmas hymns, "O Come, All Ye Faithful" rising in harmony that seemed to lift the very roof beams. Holly's clear soprano blended with her mother's gentle alto and the deeper tones of the men, creating something beautiful and unified that made her chest swell with joy.

The service continued with readings from the Gospel of Luke, the ancient words describing the journey to Bethlehem and the angels' announcement to the shepherds. Holly closed her eyes during the passages about the stable, imagining the scene her father's stories had painted so vividly—the soft animal sounds, the golden hay, the quiet miracle of new life entering the world.

But above them, unnoticed by the celebrating congregation, a single candle on the wooden rafter flickered too close to the ancient pine garland. The dry needles caught with a whisper, a tiny flame that danced for a moment before spreading to the aged timber beneath.

The fire moved silently at first, creeping along the old wood that had dried for centuries in the church's rafters. Smoke began to curl upward, still too faint to be detected over the mingled scents of pine and candle wax that already filled the air.

Holly continued singing, her voice joining the chorus of "Silent Night" that echoed through the stone walls, completely unaware that above their heads, the first tendrils of disaster were beginning to take hold. The flames found purchase in the decorative woodwork, growing bolder as they consumed the Christmas greenery that had been meant to celebrate joy and new life.

It wasn't until a woman's sharp gasp cut through the hymn that the first parishioner noticed the smoke beginning to thicken near the ceiling.

FIRE

*T*he woman's gasp pierced through "Silent Night" like a blade, and suddenly the peaceful hymn shattered into chaos. Holly watched in bewilderment as heads turned upward, eyes widening in terror at the sight of flames dancing across the ancient rafters.

"Fire!" someone screamed.

The word exploded through the congregation like a cannon shot. Peaceful Christmas Eve worship transformed into pandemonium within heartbeats. Families scrambled from their pews, gathering children and belongings in frantic haste. The gentle harmony of carols gave way to shouts of alarm, the scraping of walking sticks against stone, and the thunder of boots on ancient floors.

Holly felt her mother's arms wrap around her with fierce protectiveness, pulling her close as bodies pressed past them in the narrow aisle. Mary's embrace tightened until Holly could barely breathe, but she didn't protest—the terror in the air was palpable, thick as the smoke beginning to drift down from the ceiling.

"Stay with me, darling," Mary whispered urgently into Holly's hair. "Don't let go of my hand."

The clattering of a multitude of rushing shoes mixed with children's cries and adults' frantic calls for loved ones. Holly pressed her face against her mother's hip, overwhelmed by the cacophony of panic that had erupted around them. The church that moments before had felt like a sanctuary now seemed to close in from all sides.

Through the chaos, her father's voice rang out with calm authority.

"Everyone remain calm!" Reverend Clarke commanded from the front, his arms raised high. "Move toward the exits in an orderly fashion. Do not run—walk steadily and keep together."

His voice cut through the pandemonium like a lighthouse beam through a storm. Holly lifted her head to see him standing firm amidst the swirling confusion, his purple stole now illuminated by the orange glow spreading across the ceiling. Even as smoke thickened around him, he projected an unshakeable composure that began to steady the frightened congregation.

"Families with young children, move first," he directed, gesturing toward the main doors. "Take your time—there is room for everyone."

Sir Richard Thornhill had moved to assist, his authoritative presence helping to guide the flow of people toward safety. Holly caught a glimpse of Daniel's face across the aisle—pale with fear but moving obediently with his parents toward the exit.

Her father continued counting heads as families streamed past him, his keen eyes tracking each parishioner as they made their way to safety. Holly could see him mentally cataloguing everyone, ensuring no soul was left behind. The flames above cast dancing shadows across his determined features, but his voice never wavered.

"The Millers—yes, all accounted for. Mrs Porter with young Sarah—good. The Henshaws—"

Mary guided Holly toward the door, following the steady stream of villagers. The cold December air beckoned through the church entrance, promising escape from the choking smoke that grew thicker with each passing moment. Holly's eyes stung and watered, but she kept looking back toward her father.

The last family stumbled through the doorway into the blessed relief of winter air. Holly found herself in the church-yard, surrounded by her neighbours—all breathing heavily, all staring back at the church with expressions of shock and disbe-lief. The ancient building glowed from within now, flames visible through the stained glass windows that had moments before cast such beautiful patterns on the stone floor.

But something was wrong. Holly watched her father's face change as he conducted his final count, his methodical calm giving way to stark horror.

"Mrs Bates," he said, the words barely audible above the crackling flames. "Where is Mrs Bates?"

Holly's heart lurched. The elderly widow always sat in the back pew, often dozing during service due to her poor hearing. In the chaos and confusion, she might not have heard the alarm until it was too late.

Her father's eyes swept the churchyard desperately, hoping against hope to spot the familiar grey bonnet among the crowd. But Mrs Bates was nowhere to be seen.

The realisation hit him like a physical blow. Without hesita-tion, Reverend Clarke turned back toward the church entrance, where flames now licked hungrily at the wooden doorframe.

"Thomas, no!" Mary's scream cut through the night air.

But he was already plunging back into the inferno, his dark silhouette disappearing into the smoke-choked sanctuary. Holly watched in frozen terror as her father vanished into the orange glow, the church's interior now a writhing mass of flame and shadow.

Across the churchyard, Daniel stood transfixed beside his parents, his young face etched with horror as he witnessed this act of supreme courage. The heat radiating from the building was intense even at this distance, and everyone could see the flames spreading rapidly through the ancient timber.

Inside the church, barely visible through the smoke and fire, a figure moved with desperate purpose. Reverend Clarke battled through the superheated air, his lungs burning as he made his way toward the back pews where Mrs Bates always sat.

He found her there, hunched and bewildered, her frail hands gripping the wooden pew as she stared in confusion at the chaos around her. Her poor hearing had indeed left her unaware of the danger until the heat and smoke became over-whelming.

"Mrs Bates!" he shouted, his voice hoarse from the smoke. "Come with me—quickly now!"

She looked up at him with frightened, rheumy eyes, and he gently took her arm, supporting her trembling form as he guided her toward the exit. The journey that should have taken moments stretched into an eternity as they navigated between fallen debris and spreading flames.

They were almost to safety when Holly heard the ominous crack of splitting timber above. She watched in paralysed horror as a massive burning beam broke free from the rafters, plummeting toward the church entrance where her father and Mrs Bates struggled through the doorway.

In that final, terrible moment, Reverend Clarke made his choice. With a powerful shove, he thrust Mrs Bates forward into the safety of the churchyard just as the blazing timber crashed down behind her.

The beam caught him beneath its crushing weight, trapping

him in the doorway as flames roared around him like hungry demons. Holly's scream tore from her throat, raw and agonised, as she watched her father disappear beneath the burning wood.

Mrs Bates stumbled into the crowd, bewildered and trembling, alive because of the man now trapped behind her. The villagers pressed forward as one, desperate to help, but the heat drove them back. The entrance was completely blocked, the flames too fierce for any rescue attempt.

Holly collapsed against her mother, sobbing as the church became her father's tomb. Around them, the congregation stood in grief-stricken silence, witnessing the ultimate sacrifice of the man who had shepherded them with such devotion.

The ancient stones of St Nicholas glowed like a beacon against the winter night, but the light they cast was one of loss rather than celebration.

GOODBYE

The village had grown silent in the days since the fire. Holly pressed her face against the sitting room window, watching neighbours move through Ashford Green like shadows of their former selves. The baker's shop remained shuttered, its cheerful bell silent. Children who once filled the commons with their games now walked quietly beside their parents, their voices hushed to whispers.

Black ribbons appeared on every door, fluttering mournfully in the winter breeze. Mrs Henshaw stood with Mrs Porter by the village well, their heads bent together as they spoke in low tones about Father's courage. Even old Mr Miller, who rarely showed emotion, wiped his eyes with his sleeve as he spoke to the blacksmith about the man who had saved Mrs Bates.

Holly turned away from the window. Everything in the cottage felt wrong now—the empty chair where Father usually sat reading his sermons, the silence where his warm laughter should have been.

She found herself clinging to Mother's black dress again, her small fists twisted in the fabric as if holding on might stop the terrible emptiness from swallowing her whole. Mother's hand came down gently on her head, stroking her auburn hair with trembling fingers.

"Holly, my darling," her mother whispered, her voice barely audible. "We must dress for the service."

The funeral. Holly's stomach lurched at the thought. She understood what it meant—that Father would never come home again, never call her his little sparrow, never read scripture at their breakfast table. The knowledge sat heavy in her chest, making it hard to breathe.

Her mother moved slowly toward the wardrobe, retrieving the dark dresses that would mark this terrible day. Holly watched her mother's careful movements, noticing how she paused at Father's side of the wardrobe, her fingers brushing against his hanging coat.

"Will Father be waiting for us in heaven?" Holly asked suddenly, the question bursting from her lips before she could stop it.

Her mother knelt beside her, gathering Holly into her arms. "Yes, my precious girl. He's with God now, watching over us like the good shepherd he always was."

But Holly could see the pain flickering in her mother's eyes, the way her voice caught on the words. The cottage felt hollow around them, full of memories but empty of the man who had made it home.

Holly let Mother dress her in the unfamiliar black frock, her mind struggling to comprehend that this was real, that they were truly preparing to say goodbye forever.

SLIPPING AWAY

*T*he days following her father's funeral blurred together like watercolours in the rain. Holly found herself tiptoeing through the cottage, afraid her footsteps might shatter the fragile quiet that had settled over everything like dust.

Her mother spent most hours in her bedroom now, sitting by the window that overlooked the rose garden. The floral wallpaper that had once seemed so cheerful—pink roses climbing green trellises—now appeared faded and melancholy, as if the flowers themselves mourned alongside her. Holly would peek through the partially open door and see her mother's silhouette against the glass, her shoulders curved inward, her hands folded in her lap like broken wings.

The woman who had hummed hymns whilst arranging fresh roses seemed to have vanished entirely. Her mother's face, once animated with gentle smiles and warm laughter, had become a pale shadow. Her auburn hair hung loose and unkempt, no longer pinned up with the careful precision Holly remembered. Even her movements had changed—slow, deliberate, as if each step required tremendous effort.

Late at night, Holly pressed her ear to the thin wall between their rooms and heard the soft, muffled sounds of weeping. The sobs came in waves, sometimes quiet sniffles that barely penetrated the silence, other times deeper cries that made Holly's chest tighten with helplessness. She wanted to rush in, to crawl into Mother's bed and wrap her arms around her the way Mother had always done when Holly scraped her knees or woke from nightmares. But something held her back—a sense that Mother's grief was too vast, too deep for her small arms to encompass.

The cottage felt different now, heavy with sorrow that seemed to seep into the walls themselves. Her father's chair remained untouched, his Bible still open to the last passage he had read. Holly found herself avoiding the sitting room altogether, unable to bear the sight of his empty place.

Village friends arrived daily with offerings of kindness. Mrs Henshaw brought a steaming pot of mutton stew, her eyes red-rimmed as she pressed Holly's hand. Mrs Porter appeared with fresh bread, still warm from her oven, whilst old Mrs Whitworth shuffled up the garden path carrying a basket of preserved fruits.

"Your father was the finest man I ever knew," Mrs Henshaw whispered to Holly as she set the stew pot on the kitchen table. "He saved my Sarah from the mill pond when she was barely walking. Never forgot a kindness, never turned away a soul in need."

But when Holly carried the offerings to her mother's room, she found her staring out at the garden with vacant eyes. The food grew cold on the bedside table, untouched despite Holly's gentle encouragement.

"Mrs Henshaw brought your favourite stew," Holly would say, settling beside her Mother on the bed. "And Mrs Porter's bread—you always said she had the lightest hand with dough."

Her mother would turn slightly, offering a wan smile that

never quite reached her eyes. "That's lovely, darling. Perhaps later."

Later never came. The bread grew stale, the stew formed a skin on its surface, and Holly found herself eating alone at the kitchen table, the silence pressing against her ears.

Even when the congregation members came to pay their respects—Mr and Mrs Patterson, the young Hills, elderly Mrs Bates herself with tears streaming down her weathered cheeks — her mother received them with polite distance. She would nod and murmur appropriate responses, but Holly could see she wasn't truly present. Her spirit seemed to have followed Father somewhere Holly couldn't reach.

The visitors spoke in hushed tones about Thomas's sacrifice, about his unwavering faith, about the hole his absence had torn in their community. But their words seemed to bounce off Mother like raindrops on glass, unable to penetrate the wall of grief she had built around herself.

Holly watched it all with growing fear, sensing that something precious was slipping away with each passing day.

FINAL GIFTS

*D*ays blurred into weeks, and Holly began to understand things no ten-year-old should have to comprehend. She watched her mother's hands tremble as they reached for her teacup, noticed how her once-bright eyes had dulled to the colour of winter sky. A terrible knowing settled in Holly's chest.

"Come, Mother," Holly whispered one grey morning, slipping her small hand into her mother's pale fingers. "The roses need us."

They walked through the garden together, Holly's steps careful and measured to match her mother's faltering pace. The roses had begun their winter dormancy, their stems bare except for the crimson hips that clung like tiny jewels. Holly knelt beside the damask bush her grandmother had planted, her fingers working to clear the dead leaves that had gathered around its base.

"See how they sleep?" Holly said, glancing up at her mother hopefully. "But they're still alive underneath. You taught me that, remember? They're just waiting for spring."

Her mother stood motionless, her gaze distant and unfocused. The woman who had once shown Holly how to prune with confident, gentle strokes now seemed afraid to touch the thorny stems, as if they might cut her spirit as well as her skin.

Holly felt something shift inside her—a strange, frightening maturity that made her stomach clench. She was losing Mother too. The knowledge pressed against her ribs like a bird trying to escape, making it hard to breathe. If Mother went away like Father had, there would be no one left. No one at all.

"The garden misses you," Holly whispered, her voice smaller than she intended.

But her mother had already turned back toward the cottage, her shoulders curved like a question mark against the pewter sky.

By late February, Mother could no longer leave her bed. Holly arranged the pillows just so, ensuring her mother had the best view of the garden through the frost-etched window. She brought her father's Bible and read aloud the stories Mother had once shared with her—David and Goliath, Daniel in the lion's den, the parable of the mustard seed.

"'Though it is the smallest of all seeds,'" Holly read carefully, "'when it grows, it is the largest of garden plants.'" She looked up hopefully. "Like our roses, Mother. Small beginnings, but they grow so beautiful."

Her mother's lips curved slightly, but the smile never reached her eyes. She lay propped against the pillows, her auburn hair spread across the white linen like autumn leaves scattered by wind. Sometimes Holly caught her staring at the garden with such longing it made Holly's throat tight with unshed tears.

One slow afternoon, as pale sunlight filtered through the curtains, Mother's frail hand reached toward the bedside table where Holly had placed a single dried rose from their garden. Her fingers brushed the papery petals with infinite tenderness.

"Holly, my sweet girl," she whispered, her voice barely

audible above the settling of the house. "The garden needs tending. Remember the roses ..."

Her words trailed away like smoke, but Holly leaned closer, desperate to catch every syllable.

Three weeks later, as twilight painted the cottage walls purple, Holly sat beside her mother's bed reading Psalm Twenty-Three. Mother's breathing had grown shallow, each breath a visible effort that made Holly's own chest ache in sympathy.

Suddenly, Mother's eyes opened wide, clearer than they had been in months. Her hand found Holly's with surprising strength, fingers intertwining like the climbing roses on their garden trellis.

"Remember the roses, my darling," she whispered, tears sliding down her hollow cheeks. "Even in ashes, they bloom again. Keep faith, and God will see you through."

The words settled in the space between them, heavy with love and the terrible weight of goodbye. Holly felt them sink into her heart like seeds finding soil, knowing somehow that she would carry them forever—these final gifts from a mother who loved her beyond words, beyond breath, beyond the grave itself.

THE MORNING AFTER

*T*he next morning arrived with cruel indifference, sunlight streaming through the cottage windows as if nothing had changed. But everything had changed. Holly woke to a stillness so complete it made her ears ring. No gentle breathing from the next room, no soft rustling of sheets, no whispered prayers at dawn.

She found herself standing in the doorway of her mother's chamber, staring at the empty bed with its smoothed coverlet and plumped pillows. The dried rose still lay on the bedside table, its petals now scattered like tiny brown tears across the wood. Holly's sobs came then, quiet and broken, the sound too small for such enormous grief.

Word spread through Ashford Green like ripples on still water. Mrs Henshaw arrived first, her face streaked with tears, followed by Mrs Porter and the other village women who had loved Mother. They spoke in hushed voices about gentle Mary Clarke, remembering her kindness, her roses, her quiet grace. A second wave of sorrow crashed over the community—first their beloved reverend, now his dear wife. It seemed too much for any place to bear.

The funeral brought the entire village to the small church-yard beside the still almost desolate St Nicholas. Holly stood fragile and bird-like among the sea of black-clad mourners, clutching a bouquet of late roses she had picked that morning—pink damasks and white albas, their perfume rising like incense in the crisp air. She watched as they lowered Mother's coffin beside Father's grave, the dark earth swallowing another piece of her world.

"She taught us all what it meant to love without measure," Mrs Whitworth whispered to her neighbour.

"Such faith in the darkest hours," added Mrs Porter, dabbing her eyes.

Each kind word settled in Holly's memory beside her mother's final blessing. Even through her tears, she felt the legacy of love that surrounded her—proof that faith and kindness never truly died, but lived on in the hearts they touched.

FATED LETTER

The days following her mother's burial blurred together like watercolours in rain. Mrs Henshaw took Holly into her cottage, settling her in Sarah's small room where two narrow beds stood side by side. Sarah shared her porridge each morning and held Holly's hand when nightmares woke her, but Holly felt like a shadow moving through someone else's life.

"You're welcome here as long as needed, dear one," Mrs Henshaw assured her, smoothing Holly's tangled auburn hair. "But we must think of what's best for you."

The village women gathered in Mrs Porter's parlour to discuss Holly's future over cups of weak tea. Holly sat in the corner, pretending to read whilst their voices drifted around her like distant thunder.

"The child needs proper family," Mrs Whitworth declared, her knitting needles clicking. "She's got breeding, needs more than we can offer."

"Mary mentioned a sister once," Mrs Henshaw said slowly. "Older, married well. Lives in the next city over, Ashford, I believe."

Mrs Porter nodded. "Cordelia something-or-other. Hart, perhaps? Mary rarely spoke of her, mind you."

Holly's stomach twisted. Mother had never mentioned any sister, never spoken of relatives beyond Father and herself. The cottage had always felt complete, their little family sufficient unto itself.

"We could write," suggested Mrs Whitworth. "Explain the circumstances. Surely blood would call to blood."

The women's faces turned toward Holly with expressions of determined kindness. She forced herself to nod, though her throat felt thick with unshed tears. She wanted to cry that Rose-worth was her home, that the roses needed tending, that she belonged here among people who remembered her parents with love. But the words stuck fast.

Mrs Porter fetched writing paper from her bureau drawer.

As the women composed their careful letter—explaining the tragedy, Holly's orphaned state, and their hope for family assistance—Holly stared out the window toward Roseworth Cottage. The roses would be budding soon, pushing through winter's grip just as Mother promised. Someone else would tend them now, someone who didn't know their names or understand their stories.

The letter was sealed and dispatched that very afternoon, carrying Holly's fate toward a stranger who shared her mother's blood but none of her memories.

HART HOUSE

The carriage wheels crunched against the gravel drive as Hart House emerged from behind its towering hedgerows. Holly pressed her face to the window, her breath fogging the glass as she stared up at the imposing mansion. Three storeys of grey stone rose before her, each window gleaming like watchful eyes in the afternoon light. Elaborate chimneys pierced the sky, and ornate stonework decorated every corner and lintel.

Her small bundle of belongings felt suddenly pitiful in her lap, mainly made up of the few dresses Mrs Henshaw had helped her pack, and a blue dress of her mothers'. The cottage seemed a lifetime away, though barely two weeks had passed since the funeral.

The carriage door opened with a sharp click. Holly stepped down onto the circular drive, her worn boots silent against the perfectly maintained gravel. Each stone seemed placed with deliberate precision, unlike the meandering path that led to Roseworth's front door.

Heavy oak doors swung open before she could knock. A

butler in pristine livery bowed stiffly, his expression revealing nothing as he gestured her inside. Holly's footsteps echoed in the vast entrance hall, the sound swallowed by soaring ceilings and dark wooden panels that stretched upward into shadow.

Portraits lined the walls—stern-faced men in military dress, elegant ladies with jewelled necks, children posed with hunting dogs or elaborate toys. Their painted eyes seemed to follow her movement, weighing and measuring this small intruder in their ancestral domain. Heavy burgundy drapery framed tall windows, blocking much of the natural light and casting everything in muted tones of gold and amber.

"My dear child!"

The voice rang across the marble floor like crystal striking stone. Holly turned to see a tall woman descending the grand staircase, her dark blonde hair arranged in an elaborate coiffure, her sapphire gown rustling with each calculated step. Cold blue eyes fixed upon Holly with an intensity that made her stomach flutter.

"Sweet Holly, at last we meet." Lady Cordelia Hart swept forward, her movements graceful yet predatory. She reached for Holly's hands, her fingers cool and firm as they clasped her small ones. "How you favour dear Mary—the same auburn hair, the same delicate features."

Holly tried to curtsy as her mother had taught her, but Cordelia's grip held her steady.

"Such terrible tragedy," Cordelia continued, her voice dropping to a sympathetic murmur. "Your poor mother, taken so soon after your father's heroic sacrifice. I am devastated we could not attend the services—Geoffrey was dreadfully ill with influenza, and I dared not leave his side. We sent a letter explaining."

The explanation felt rehearsed, like lines memorised for a play. Holly nodded politely, though something cold settled in her chest. Her mother had never mentioned illness keeping anyone away.

"Come, you must be exhausted from your journey." Cordelia's hand settled on Holly's shoulder, steering her toward an adjoining room. "We shall have tea, and you can tell me everything about your dear mother's final days."

The drawing room overwhelmed Holly's senses. Gilt-framed mirrors reflected endless images of opulent furniture—velvet settees with carved mahogany legs, tables inlaid with mother-of-pearl, crystal decanters catching fragments of light from an enormous chandelier. Fresh hothouse flowers arranged in silver vases filled the air with an almost cloying sweetness.

"Sit here beside me, darling." Cordelia patted a silk cushion. "You must think me terribly grand after your simple cottage, but I want you to feel quite at home."

Holly perched on the edge of the settee, her hands folded carefully in her lap. The fabric felt slippery beneath her fingers, nothing like the worn chintz chairs where she'd learned her letters.

"Such a bright child you appear to be," Cordelia observed, her gaze appraising. "Mary always spoke of your quick mind and gentle spirit in her letters. Though I confess we corresponded so rarely—sisters often drift apart when life takes different paths."

The admission hung in the air like incense, sweet but somehow suffocating. Holly wanted to ask about these letters, about why her mother had never mentioned them, but uncertainty kept her silent.

The door opened with a soft creak, admitting a portly gentleman with thinning brown hair and grey eyes that darted nervously around the room. His cravat sat askew, and he fumbled with it as he approached.

"Ah, Geoffrey!" Cordelia's voice sharpened almost impercep-tibly. "Come meet our dear Holly."

Sir Geoffrey Hart shuffled forward, his movements hesitant. "Yes, of course. Terrible business about your parents, child. Quite terrible indeed."

He offered a brief bow, his eyes sliding away from Holly's face to fix on the Persian carpet beneath their feet. When Cordelia cleared her throat pointedly, he startled slightly.

"Perhaps you might ring for tea, Geoffrey?"

"Certainly, my dear. At once." He moved toward the bell pull with evident relief, his fingers trembling slightly as he tugged the silk cord.

Holly watched this exchange with growing unease. Something in the way Geoffrey's shoulders hunched, the manner in which his voice dropped when addressing his wife, reminded her of a scolded child rather than the master of such a grand house. His weakness seemed to fill the room like a tangible presence, making Holly wonder how he might treat an unwanted guest—a reminder of family obligations he appeared incapable of shouldering.

"Now then," Cordelia said, her smile returning full force, "we shall make you quite comfortable here. Such a blessing to have family close, don't you think?"

That evening, after a supper of roasted fowl and delicate pastries that sat heavily in her stomach, Holly found herself alone in the corridors of Hart House. The butler had shown her to a small chamber on the second floor, but sleep eluded her. The unfamiliar sounds of the grand house—creaking floorboards, settling timbers, the distant chiming of a clock—kept her restless.

She slipped from her room, her bare feet silent on the polished wood floors. Gas lamps flickered along the walls, casting dancing shadows that made the ancestral portraits seem to watch her progress with disapproving eyes.

Everything gleamed with careful attention. Mahogany tables bore arrangements of porcelain figurines—shepherdesses with rosy cheeks, hunting dogs frozen mid-leap, delicate flowers wrought in painted clay. Holly traced her finger along a gilt picture frame, marvelling at its intricate scrollwork. At Roseworth, their few precious items had been simple and well-loved.

Here, beauty felt calculated rather than cherished. Chinese vases stood like sentries on marble pedestals. Persian carpets stretched beneath her feet, their patterns so complex they made her dizzy. Crystal chandeliers hung overhead like frozen waterfalls, each prism catching fragments of gaslight and scattering them into rainbow shards.

Holly paused before a display case filled with silver—tea services that gleamed like mirrors, candlesticks twisted into elaborate shapes, serving platters engraved with the Hart family crest. The sheer quantity overwhelmed her. How many villages could such wealth feed? How many children like those at the autumn fair could be clothed and sheltered?

The house pressed down upon her with its expectations. Every surface whispered of money carefully spent to impress, of appearances maintained at tremendous cost. She thought of Cordelia's careful words at supper, how she'd mentioned the "burden" of keeping up Hart House, the "sacrifices" required of their position in society.

Holly shivered, though the corridor was warm. Something in the way Cordelia's eyes had assessed her during their conversation, calculating and measuring, made her feel less like a beloved niece and more like an unwelcome complication. The grandeur that surrounded her felt less like generosity and more like a stage set—beautiful, expensive, and utterly without warmth.

She hurried back to her chamber, suddenly desperate for the safety of closed doors. Holly couldn't shake the sensation that she'd become another ornament in Cordelia's carefully curated collection—valuable, perhaps, but only for what she might be worth.

IN PRIVATE

$\mathcal{A}$ week passed before Holly witnessed Cordelia's first gathering—a ladies' tea that filled the drawing room with rustling silk and musical laughter. Holly remained upstairs during the festivities, though she could hear the animated chatter drifting through the floorboards.

"Such a devoted aunt," one voice proclaimed. "Taking in that poor orphaned child."

"Lady Hart has always possessed the most generous spirit," another agreed. "Despite her own trials."

Holly pressed her ear to the floor, catching fragments of praise for Cordelia's selfless charity. The voices painted her aunt as a paragon of virtue, a woman who opened her heart and home without hesitation.

When the last carriage wheels faded into the distance, Holly crept to the top of the stairs. Below, servants cleared away delicate teacups and removed wilted flower arrangements. Cordelia stood in the doorway, her smile dissolving like sugar in rain.

"Put those away properly," she snapped at a maid struggling with a silver tray. "I won't have you chipping the good china with your clumsiness."

The warmth that had charmed her guests vanished entirely. Cordelia's voice carried the sharp edge of a blade, cutting through the house's earlier harmony. Holly shrank back against the banister.

"Holly." Cordelia's call rang up the stairwell. "Come down at once."

Holly descended slowly, watching her aunt's face remain fixed in its new, colder expression. The woman who had cooed over her guests' compliments now regarded Holly with barely concealed irritation.

"You'll take your supper in your room tonight," Cordelia declared. "I'm far too exhausted to endure chatter at the dining table."

Holly's room—if it could be called that—sat tucked beneath the servants' stairs. She had only gotten to sleep in the luxurious room upstairs for two nights. Barely larger than the pantry at Roseworth, this new room contained a narrow bed, a wash-stand, and a single chair. The window faced north, admitting precious little light even during the brightest days. A thin blanket provided the only protection against the persistent chill that seeped through the walls.

The evening meal consisted of cold mutton and bread that had seen better days. Holly ate in silence, listening to the house settle around her. When darkness fell completely, she blew out her single candle and tried to find comfort in the lumpy mattress.

Voices drifted through the thin walls—Cordelia and Geoffrey, their conversation growing more heated with each exchange.

"The girl possesses everything," Cordelia's voice cut through the plaster. "A fortune she doesn't even comprehend, sitting there like some pathetic waif."

"She's only a child, Cordelia," Geoffrey's weaker tones protested. "Surely we can—"

"Can what? Continue bleeding money we don't possess?" The scorn in Cordelia's voice made Holly flinch. "Mary inherited Grandmother's entire estate while I received nothing. Nothing, Geoffrey. And now this slip of a girl holds what should rightfully belong to our family."

Holly pressed her hands against her ears, but the words penetrated anyway.

"The estate remains in trust until she reaches majority," Geoffrey mumbled. "There's nothing we can—"

"There are always options," Cordelia interrupted, her voice dropping to a whisper Holly had to strain to hear.

Holly couldn't hear what Cordelia said next, her voice too low.

"Cordelia, surely you don't mean—"

"I mean we cannot allow sentiment to destroy our future," she hissed. "I've sacrificed everything to maintain our position in society. I won't watch it crumble because of one inconvenient orphan."

Holly lay frozen beneath her thin blanket, understanding finally settling over her like ice water. The sweet aunt who had welcomed her with tears and embraces existed only for public consumption. In private, she had become something far crueller.

CRUEL NORMALCY

*T*he dining room table stretched like a chasm between Holly and the feast laid out each evening. Crystal goblets caught the candlelight, reflecting prismatic rainbows across polished mahogany, while silver serving dishes displayed roasted pheasant, buttered vegetables, and cream-laden puddings. Holly's place setting occupied the far end, where a chipped plate held portions that wouldn't satisfy a sparrow.

Tonight, a single slice of bread accompanied a spoonful of watery soup that had clearly been thinned from the kitchen's dregs. Holly lifted her spoon with careful precision, aware that Cordelia watched her every movement with hawk-like intensity.

"My dear child," Cordelia's voice carried across the expanse with false sweetness. "You're picking at your food like a timid bird. We mustn't let you waste away in this large house."

The cruel smile that accompanied these words made Holly's stomach clench tighter than hunger ever could. Geoffrey shifted uncomfortably in his chair, his attention fixed on cutting his portion of roasted fowl into unnecessarily small pieces.

"Perhaps you're simply not accustomed to proper meals,"

Cordelia continued, delicately sipping her wine. "Village fare tends toward the ... rustic, doesn't it?"

Holly remembered her mother's warm kitchen, where fresh bread emerged from the oven each morning and stews bubbled with vegetables from their own garden. Those meals had nourished both body and spirit, shared with laughter and stories around their small wooden table. This grand dining room, with its towering walls and echoing silence, felt more like a mausoleum than a place for sustenance.

"I'm grateful for whatever you provide, Aunt Cordelia," Holly managed, the words scraping against her throat.

"Of course you are, dear one. Of course you are."

Morning brought new humiliations disguised as necessity. Cordelia appeared in Holly's cramped quarters before dawn, carrying a bucket and scrubbing brush.

"You'll start with the entrance hall," she announced, setting the implements beside Holly's narrow bed. "The floors have grown quite neglected, and we can't have guests thinking we maintain slovenly standards."

Holly's knees protested against the cold marble as she worked her way across the expansive floor. The brush left her palms raw and bleeding, but she dared not complain. Above her, the Hart family portraits seemed to sneer down with disapproval, their painted eyes following her degraded progress.

Water sloshed over the bucket's rim as Holly carried it up the servants' stairs to empty and refill. Her arms ached from the weight, and her back screamed from hours spent bent over the brush. The elegant ladies who visited Cordelia would never guess that their hostess's orphaned niece crawled across these same floors like a common scullery maid.

Afternoons brought mending baskets overflowing with Cordelia's finest gowns. Holly squinted by candlelight, struggling to repair torn seams and replace missing buttons on garments that cost more than most families earned in a year.

Her fingers, once nimble with embroidery under her mother's patient guidance, now cramped and bled from the endless needlework.

"Mind you don't stain the silk," Cordelia warned, examining Holly's work with critical eyes. "These gowns require the most delicate touch. I suppose village needlework involves rougher materials."

Each task felt designed to break something inside her—not just her body, but her spirit. Holly found herself moving through the days like a ghost, performing her duties with mechanical precision while her thoughts drifted to Roseworth's rose garden. She could almost smell the damask blooms her grandmother had planted, could almost hear her mother's gentle humming as they worked side by side.

Weeks blended into months with chilling normalcy. Cordelia maintained her public facade of devoted aunt, receiving visitors who praised her Christian charity in taking on such a burden. Behind closed doors, however, her manipulations grew more subtle and sinister.

"Geoffrey, I worry about the child," she remarked one evening as Holly cleared their dinner plates. "She seems so ... fragile. Perhaps proper guidance would benefit her constitution."

Holly's hands trembled as she stacked the china, recognising the calculated tone in her aunt's voice.

"What sort of guidance?" Geoffrey asked, though his question carried little conviction.

"Professional care. There are establishments that specialise in helping troubled young minds find their proper place in society."

The plates rattled in Holly's grasp. She steadied them quickly, hoping her reaction had gone unnoticed.

"She's grieving, Cordelia. Time will—"

"Time, my dear husband, is precisely what we cannot afford

to squander. The longer we delay proper intervention, the more difficult her ... adjustment becomes."

Holly escaped to the kitchen, her pulse hammering against her ribs. Whatever Cordelia planned, it would not involve kindness or genuine care. The woman who had transformed her into an unpaid servant was plotting something far worse than domestic humiliation.

BRANDY

Geoffrey's brandy glass trembled against his lips as Cordelia's words settled into the drawing room's oppressive silence. The fire crackled in the grate, casting dancing shadows across her composed features, but her eyes remained cold as winter stone.

"You know, Geoffrey, if the child were to slip away before her twenty-first birthday ..."

The sentence hung unfinished between them, its implications coiling through the air like smoke. Geoffrey set down his glass with excessive care, as though the crystal might shatter under the weight of what his wife had just suggested.

"Cordelia, surely you don't mean—"

"I mean nothing more than what nature might provide," she replied, smoothing her skirt with practised elegance. "Young people are so very fragile, particularly those weakened by grief and ... unfortunate circumstances."

Geoffrey's stomach churned. Through the drawing room's doorway, he could see Holly in the corridor, carrying yet another bucket of scrubbing water. The child moved like a wraith, her small frame bent under burdens no ten-year-old should bear. Her auburn hair, once bright as autumn leaves, now hung limp and dull around shoulders that seemed to grow thinner each passing day.

"Perhaps we should ease her duties," he ventured, his voice barely rising above a whisper. "Show more ... Christian compassion."

Cordelia's laugh tinkled like breaking glass. "Compassion? My dear husband, we have shown remarkable compassion by taking in Mary's orphaned brat at all."

Geoffrey flinched at the venom in her tone. This wasn't the woman he'd married—or perhaps it was, and he'd simply been too blind to see beneath her social veneer. The woman who smiled so sweetly at garden parties and charitable gatherings revealed her true nature only within these walls.

"The child has lost everything," he tried again, though conviction drained from his words like water through cracked stone.

Cordelia rose from her chair with fluid grace, crossing to where Geoffrey sat slumped in defeat. Her perfume, usually so alluring, now seemed cloying as she leaned close to his ear.

"Would you have us lose Hart House, Geoffrey?" Her breath was warm against his skin, but her words froze his blood. "That child has everything—she doesn't even know the fortune at risk."

Geoffrey's hands clenched around the brandy glass. Their creditors grew more insistent each week, their polite letters becoming increasingly sharp demands. The gambling debts he'd accumulated during those foolish nights at the gentlemen's club now threatened to destroy everything they'd built.

"Your investments," Cordelia continued, her voice a silken whisper, "have left us rather ... exposed. The trust fund that should have been mine by rights now sits waiting for a child who may not survive to claim it."

The brandy burned his throat, but not enough to wash away

the bitter taste of his wife's words. He thought of Holly's green eyes—so like her mother's—and how they'd dulled from their initial wariness to something approaching despair.

"She's just a child, Cordelia."

"She's an obstacle." Cordelia's fingers traced across his shoulder, a gesture that once would have comforted but now felt predatory. "Every day she draws breath in this house is another day our financial ruin draws closer."

Geoffrey stared into the amber depths of his brandy, watching the liquid swirl as Cordelia's fingers continued their calculated caress across his shoulders.

"You must understand the injustice of it all," she murmured, her voice taking on the wounded tone she wielded so expertly. "When Grandmother penned that dreadful will, she favoured Mary simply because she was born of the second marriage."

Her hand tightened on his shoulder. "I was the elder daughter, Geoffrey. I cared for that woman through her final illness, read to her, tended her needs. Yet because of some legal technicality regarding my father's first marriage, everything passed to my half-sister."

Geoffrey remembered Mary Clarke's gentle nature, so different from the woman now standing behind him. "Mary never flaunted her inheritance—"

"Mary never needed to," Cordelia snapped, her composure cracking momentarily. "She had it all—the cottage, the trust fund, even that simpering devotion from Thomas Clarke. Meanwhile, we struggle to maintain our position, to keep up appearances that our very survival depends upon."

She moved to face him directly, her blue eyes blazing with years of suppressed resentment. "That child sleeps above stairs whilst we teeter on the edge of ruin. Roseworth Cottage and its trust fund sit waiting for her twenty-first birthday—wealth that should rightfully be mine."

Geoffrey reached for the decanter with shaking hands,

pulling away from his wife's grip. He poured himself another measure of amber liquid. The alcohol had become his refuge from the mounting pressure of their circumstances, the only thing that silenced the voice in his head screaming that this was wrong.

"The household accidents," he began, then stopped himself. He didn't want to hear the answer.

"Accidents happen so frequently to careless children," Cordelia said, returning to her chair as though they'd been discussing the weather. "Loose stones on stairs. Frayed ropes at wells. Food that's perhaps turned without anyone noticing."

Geoffrey's stomach lurched, and he emptied his glass in one burning gulp. The weight of complicity settled on his shoulders like a lead cloak. Each nod he gave, each weak protest he failed to voice, made him party to whatever dark schemes his wife was weaving.

Holly passed by the doorway again, this time carrying mending to her cramped quarters. She moved so quietly, as though afraid to disturb the very air around her.

Cordelia watched his gaze follow the child. "Well, my dear husband? Shall we continue showing our ... charitable nature?"

Geoffrey nodded glumly, hating himself for the gesture, and reached once more for the brandy.

A PROMISE TO THE ROSES

*T*he evening air carried a chill that bit through Holly's thin shawl as she slipped from the servants' entrance into Hart House's forgotten corners. Her duties were complete —the floors scrubbed raw, the silver polished until it gleamed, the mending finished by candlelight that had left her eyes aching. Yet sleep eluded her in that cramped chamber beneath the stairs, where Cordelia's whispered conversations with Geoffrey filtered through the thin walls like poison.

Behind the grand house lay a patch of ground that might once have been a proper garden. Weeds choked the pathways, and ivy strangled what remained of ornamental hedges. But there, tucked against the rear wall where moonlight touched neglected soil, Holly glimpsed something that made her heart leap.

Roses.

Wild and untended, their canes had grown long and thorny, climbing the stone wall in desperate search of light. But they lived still, their blooms pale in the darkness yet unmistakably sweet with that fragrance Holly knew better than her own breath.

She approached carefully, mindful of the thorns that caught at her patched dress. The scent grew stronger—damask roses, like those her mother had tended with such devotion. Holly reached out with trembling fingers to touch one perfect bloom, its petals soft as silk against her work-roughened skin.

"Even in ashes, they bloom again."

Her mother's final words whispered through the garden like a benediction. Holly closed her eyes, breathing deeply of that beloved fragrance, and felt something shift inside her chest. Not the crushing despair that had weighted her days since arriving at Hart House, but something fiercer. Something that tasted of defiance.

These roses had survived neglect, drought, and the choking embrace of weeds. They had found purchase in poor soil and climbed toward whatever light they could reach. They had endured.

Just as she would endure.

Holly knelt beside the largest bush, her fingers working carefully to clear away the worst of the weeds from its base. The work was gentle—nothing like the harsh scrubbing Cordelia demanded—and with each handful of bindweed she pulled away, the roses seemed to breathe more freely.

"I won't let her break me," Holly whispered to the flowers, her voice steady despite the tears that slipped down her cheeks. "Whatever she's planning, whatever cruelties she devises, I won't give her the satisfaction."

The roses rustled in response to a night breeze, their thorns catching the moonlight like tiny daggers. Holly understood their message. Beauty required protection. Survival demanded sharp edges.

She thought of her father's courage in that burning church, of her mother's gentle strength through grief and illness. Their daughter would not cower in corners, would not fade away like some wraith haunting Hart House corridors. She was Holly

Clarke, raised on faith and roses, taught that love could triumph over the darkest circumstances.

Cordelia might control her days, might assign her the harshest tasks and deny her proper food, but she could not touch what mattered most. Holly's memories of Roseworth remained untainted. Her parents' teachings lived on in her heart. And somewhere beyond Hart House's oppressive walls, the cottage waited with its gardens full of promise.

Holly rose from the garden, brushing soil from her knees. Tomorrow would bring fresh cruelties, new humiliations designed to crush her spirit. But tonight, surrounded by the perfume of wild roses and strengthened by their example, she made herself a promise.

She would be clever where Cordelia was cruel. Patient where her aunt was hasty. She would watch and listen and learn, gathering whatever knowledge might protect her from the shadows gathering around Hart House.

Most importantly, she would survive.

The roses had shown her how.

STONES

*T*he January frost had turned the stone steps leading from the kitchen into treacherous territory, each step slick with ice that gleamed like polished glass. Holly gripped the heavy bucket of wash water, her fingers already numb despite the rough wool mittens that barely covered her knuckles. The lye soap stung where it had splashed onto her cracked skin, but she dared not pause—Cordelia expected these steps scrubbed before the morning callers arrived.

Holly lowered herself carefully onto the top step, the bucket balanced against her hip as she reached for the coarse brush. The stone beneath her foot shifted.

Time slowed as her boot found nothing but air where solid ground should have been. The loose stone tilted sideways, her ankle twisting sharply as she fought for balance. The bucket flew from her grasp, soap water cascading down the steps as Holly tumbled backward, her spine striking each stone edge with bruising force.

She landed in a heap at the bottom, breath knocked from her lungs and pain shooting through her ribs like lightning. The empty bucket clanged against the stones beside her head, its metallic ring echoing through the courtyard. Holly lay stunned, ice-cold water soaking through her thin dress as she struggled to draw air into her burning chest.

"Holly! Oh, my dear child!"

Cordelia's voice rang out across the courtyard, sharp with apparent alarm. Holly heard the rapid tap of heeled boots on stone as her aunt hurried from the house, her morning dress rustling with each purposeful step.

Holly pushed herself upright, wincing as her bruised ribs protested. Her left wrist throbbed where she'd thrown it out to break her fall, and something warm trickled down her forehead. She touched the spot gingerly, her fingers coming away stained with blood.

"What on earth happened?" Cordelia knelt beside her, but her hands hovered without quite touching, as though Holly might somehow contaminate her fine wool dress. "Are you hurt badly?"

Holly studied her aunt's face, searching for genuine concern in those pale blue eyes. What she found instead was something that made her stomach clench with fresh fear. Behind the mask of worry lurked a gleam of satisfaction, quickly suppressed but unmistakable.

"I ... the stone moved," Holly managed, her voice barely above a whisper, "when I stepped on it."

"How dreadfully careless of you," Cordelia chided, rising to examine the offending step. She prodded the loose stone with the toe of her leather boot, watching it rock back and forth on its unstable foundation. "These old houses require such careful maintenance. One can never be too cautious."

Holly struggled to her feet, her wet dress clinging uncomfortably to her legs. The cut on her forehead stung in the cold air, and her wrist had begun to swell. "I didn't know it was loose."

"Of course you didn't." Cordelia's tone carried no warmth,

despite her words. "We simply must be more careful in the future. These accidents can be so ... unfortunate."

The way she lingered on that final word sent ice through Holly's veins that had nothing to do with the January weather. Holly bobbed a hasty curtsey, gathering the scattered cleaning supplies with trembling hands.

"Clean yourself up before the callers arrive," Cordelia instructed, already turning back toward the house. "And do try to be more mindful. We can't have you falling and injuring yourself properly."

Three weeks later, the well rope snapped.

ROPES

*H*olly had noticed the fraying strands that morning as she lowered the bucket into the dark depths. The hemp was old, its fibres split and weakened where they rubbed against the stone lip of the well. She'd mentioned it to Mrs Dawes, the cook, who'd merely shrugged and muttered something about making do with what they had.

The bucket descended smoothly enough, disappearing into the shadows with a distant splash. Holly began the careful process of hauling it back up, hand over hand, the rope rough against her palms even through her worn gloves. The water sloshed heavily as it rose, forty pounds of liquid that would need to last the scullery through the afternoon's washing.

The rope parted with a sound like a pistol shot.

Holly's hands flew upward as the tension vanished, the sudden release sending her staggering backward. The bucket plummeted into darkness, its crash echoing up from the depths like thunder. Water erupted from the well's mouth, drenching Holly from head to toe in freezing spray that drove the breath from her lungs.

She stood gasping in the courtyard, her dress sodden and

her heart hammering against her ribs. The frayed end of rope dangled uselessly over the well's edge, its broken fibres catching the weak winter sunlight.

"Holly! What was that dreadful noise?"

Cordelia emerged from the morning room, her embroidery still clutched in one pale hand. She surveyed the scene—Holly dripping wet, the severed rope, the spreading puddle of well water—with an expression of theatrical dismay.

"Oh dear! Are you all right, child?" She approached with measured steps, careful to avoid the worst of the flooding. "Whatever happened?"

"The rope broke." Holly's teeth chattered as she spoke, the wet fabric of her dress beginning to freeze in the bitter air. "It was frayed, and it snapped when the bucket was nearly up."

"How dreadful!" Cordelia examined the broken rope, turning the end over in her gloved fingers. "These old fixtures are so unreliable. Thank goodness you weren't leaning over the well when it happened. You might have fallen in."

Again, that peculiar glitter in her aunt's eyes, quickly masked by a show of concern. Holly wrapped her arms around herself, shivering violently as the wind cut through her soaked clothing.

"You must get out of those wet things immediately," Cordelia continued, though she made no move to help. "We can't have you catching your death of cold."

The phrase hung in the air between them, innocent enough on its surface but weighted with implications that made Holly's skin crawl. She curtsied hastily and fled toward the servants' entrance, her wet boots squishing with each step.

Behind her, she heard Cordelia calling for Geoffrey, her voice carrying clearly across the courtyard.

"We really must see about replacing this rope, dear. Before someone has a proper accident."

Holly didn't look back, but she could feel her aunt's gaze boring into her spine like a blade. The accidents weren't random—she was certain of it now. The loose stone, conveniently positioned where Holly would step. The frayed rope, left untended despite its obvious danger.

Someone wanted her hurt.

Someone wanted her dead.

OBLIVION

Geoffrey sat hunched over his mahogany desk, the crystal tumbler cradled between his trembling palms. The brandy caught the firelight, amber liquid swirling in lazy circles as he turned the glass around and around. Each revolution mirrored the churning in his stomach, the sick twist of knowledge he could no longer push away.

The rope had been fraying for weeks. He'd seen it himself during his morning walks through the courtyard, noticed the way the hemp fibres split and curled where they rubbed against the stone. He'd meant to replace it—had even mentioned it to Cordelia once over dinner.

"Oh, that old thing will hold a while longer," she'd said, cutting her lamb with surgical precision. "No sense spending money unnecessarily."

Now the crash from the well still echoed in his ears, followed by Cordelia's voice floating through the window. *Before someone has a proper accident.* The words made his skin crawl.

Geoffrey lifted the tumbler to his lips, the brandy burning a familiar path down his throat. It tasted of shame and cowardice, but it dulled the sharp edges of what he was becoming. What he'd already become.

Holly's footsteps had passed his study window minutes ago —quick, frightened patters as she fled toward the servants' entrance. He'd glimpsed her through the glass, soaked to the bone and shivering like a wounded sparrow. Ten years old and orphaned, reduced to scurrying through his house like a ghost.

The child who should have been sleeping in silk sheets and learning French was instead scrubbing floors until her hands bled. The heiress to Roseworth Cottage was hauling water from wells with rotting ropes.

Geoffrey's hand shook as he reached for the decanter. The crystal clinked against crystal, a delicate sound that reminded him of better days, when his conscience had been clean and his wife's smile genuine.

But those days belonged to a different man—one who hadn't nodded along to whispered conversations about household accidents. One who hadn't watched a grieving child grow thinner by the week and done nothing to stop it.

He'd told himself it was temporary. That Cordelia simply needed time to adjust to their changed circumstances. That Holly's presence was indeed a burden they could ill afford.

All lies, and he knew it.

The truth sat in his gut like poison: every frayed rope, every loose stone, every day he said nothing made him complicit. Made him a willing participant in whatever Cordelia had planned.

Geoffrey drained his glass and immediately refilled it, seeking oblivion in the bottom of the bottle.

QUIET DETERMINATION

*H*olly descended the narrow servant's stairs, her damp dress clinging to her trembling frame. Each step felt heavier than the last, the weight of another "accident" pressing down upon her shoulders like a stone. The corridor stretched before her, dimly lit by a single flickering lamp that cast dancing shadows on the peeling wallpaper.

Her small room waited at the end—barely larger than a cupboard, with a single window that overlooked the alley where refuse bins gathered like silent sentinels. The thin mattress sagged beneath her as she sank onto its edge, pulling the threadbare blanket around her shoulders.

The cold seeped through the walls, through her bones, settling deep in her chest where grief lived alongside growing fear. Holly pressed her fingers against the floorboard beneath her bed, feeling for the loose edge she'd discovered weeks ago. Her fingertips found the familiar groove, and she pried up the board with careful precision.

Nestled in the hollow space lay her most precious possession —a small leather Bible, its pages worn soft with age. Mrs Dawes had pressed it into her hands during her first month at Hart

House, when Holly's tears had fallen into the dishwater she'd been scrubbing dishes with.

"This belonged to my dear mother," the cook had whispered, glancing over her shoulder toward the main house. "She'd want it to go to someone who needs its comfort."

Holly lifted the Bible with reverent hands, feeling the familiar weight of its promise. The leather cover bore the imprint of countless fingers, the gold lettering faded but still legible in the moonlight streaming through her window.

She opened to a page marked with a pressed violet—one of the last flowers from Roseworth's garden, picked before she'd left her childhood home. The delicate petals had turned brown, but their fragrance lingered faintly between the pages of Psalms.

"Weeping may endure for a night, but joy cometh in the morning," she read silently, her lips moving with each word. The verses flowed over her like cool water on parched earth, washing away the taste of fear that lingered from the well rope's snap.

Holly closed her eyes, letting the Bible rest open in her lap. In the darkness behind her eyelids, she could see Mother kneeling in the rose garden, her gentle hands pruning the thorny stems with infinite care. The memory bloomed with startling clarity—Mother's auburn hair catching the morning light, her soft humming drifting on the breeze.

"Even in ashes, they bloom again," Holly whispered, her mother's final words echoing in the cramped room like a prayer. The phrase wrapped around her heart, warm and steady, pushing back against the cold that tried to claim her spirit.

She could almost hear her mother's voice, feel the gentle touch of her fingers smoothing Holly's hair. The love in that memory burned brighter than any gas lamp, more warming than any fire Cordelia might allow in the grand rooms below.

"Keep faith, and God will see you through," Holly murmured, her voice growing stronger with each syllable. The words tasted of hope, of roses blooming wild in forgotten gardens, of promises kept even when the world turned cruel.

Her resolve crystallised like frost on glass, beautiful and unbreakable. Cordelia might control her days, might orchestrate her accidents and steal her inheritance, but she could not touch this sanctuary Holly carried within herself.

The Bible's pages rustled as Holly turned to another passage, seeking comfort in the familiar rhythms of scripture. Outside her window, Ashford's gaslights flickered like distant stars, and somewhere beyond them lay Roseworth Cottage, waiting patiently for her return.

Holly smiled in the darkness, her spirit kindling with quiet determination.

WARMTH

The morning air bit through Holly's threadbare shawl as she trudged along the cobbled streets toward Ashford's bustling market square. Her thirteenth birthday had come and gone without acknowledgement at Hart House. The basket of eggs in her arms felt heavier with each step, though it contained barely a dozen—all Cordelia deemed fit to spare from the household stores.

Holly understood the game perfectly now. First it had been old linens, then tarnished spoons, followed by withered vegetables from the kitchen garden. Each errand sent her deeper into the rougher quarters of town, where pickpockets lurked and cart wheels flew dangerously close to small figures darting between stalls.

If the streets didn't claim her, at least Cordelia profited.

Holly bit her tongue against the bitter taste of resentment and pressed on.

The market bloomed before her like a tapestry of colour and sound. Vendors called out their wares in cheerful voices that rang across the square, their stalls draped in bright canvas and overflowing with autumn's bounty. The scent of fresh bread drifted from the baker's cart, mingling with the earthy smell of turnips and the sweet perfume of late apples. Holly's stomach clenched with familiar hunger as she passed a pie seller's stand, the golden pastries still steaming from the oven.

She found an empty spot near the fountain's edge and set her wooden crate down with careful precision. The basket looked pitifully small atop its makeshift perch, the pale eggs nestled in wisps of straw that had seen better days. Holly arranged them with gentle fingers, ensuring each one caught what sunlight filtered through the morning clouds.

"Fresh eggs," she called softly, her voice barely rising above the market's din. A group of housewives bustled past without a glance, their shopping baskets already brimming with purchases from more established vendors. Holly tried again, raising her voice slightly. "Fresh eggs from Hart House."

The lie tasted bitter on her tongue. These eggs came from the servants' quarter of the hen yard, the ones Cordelia deemed unfit for her own table. But Holly had learned to swallow such small deceptions if they meant a few extra coins for Cordelia's purse.

A well-dressed family approached the fountain, their children laughing as they chased each other between the market stalls. The mother's fur-trimmed cloak rustled as she walked, her husband's gold watch chain catching the light. Holly watched them with a hollow ache in her chest, remembering walks through this very market with her own parents, their hands warm in hers as they selected treats for Sunday tea.

"Eggs, ma'am?" Holly ventured as the woman drew near. But the lady's gaze swept over Holly's patched dress and hollow cheeks without pause, steering her children away with a subtle shift of her body.

Holly's shoulders sagged. She pulled her shawl tighter, feeling the weight of curious stares from other vendors who recognised her as the strange girl from Hart House—the one who sold scraps and cast-offs while her aunt entertained society ladies in silk gowns.

The morning crawled forward with painful slowness. Holly sold three eggs to a kitchen maid she recognised from one of the neighbouring estates, and another two to an elderly man who took pity on her obvious desperation. Each transaction brought barely enough coins to jingle in her palm, far short of what Cordelia would expect upon her return.

Through the shifting crowd, Holly caught sight of a tall young man approaching from the direction of the bookshop. His dark coat marked him as gentry, and leather-bound volumes tucked beneath his arm suggested a student home from his studies. Something about his careful, measured gait stirred a memory she couldn't quite grasp.

He drew closer, and Holly found herself looking up into a pair of dark brown eyes that seemed startlingly familiar. The young man had grown tall and refined, his jaw more defined than she remembered, but those eyes—

"Miss Clarke?" he asked, his voice carrying a note of shock that made her heart skip. "Holly Clarke?"

The name struck her like a distant church bell, echoing through years of fear and servitude. Holly's brow furrowed as she searched his face, trying to place the kindness she saw there amidst the fragments of her childhood memories. Before she could form words, recognition bloomed in her chest like a flower opening to sunlight.

Those were the eyes that had watched her climb apple trees. The hands that had offered a pristine handkerchief when she'd scraped her knee. The boy who had visited Roseworth with his father, who had listened to her chatter about roses and cats with patient attention.

Tears welled in Holly's green eyes without warning, a storm of emotions crashing over her like waves against a crumbling seawall. Relief and sorrow tangled together in her throat, three years of accumulated loneliness suddenly given voice by this unexpected kindness. She looked up at him through her tears, seeing past the polished gentleman to the gentle boy who had once given her his most prized possession.

"Daniel," she whispered, his name feeling foreign on her lips after so long.

"Yes." His voice softened with infinite tenderness. "Yes, it's Daniel."

He stepped closer to her makeshift stall, his gaze taking in the meagre display of eggs, her patched dress, the shadows beneath her eyes. Holly watched his expression shift from surprise to something that looked dangerously close to anger—not at her, but for her.

Without hesitation, Daniel reached into his coat and withdrew his purse. "I'll take them all," he said quietly, his fingers counting out coins with deliberate care. "Every egg you have."

Holly stared as silver pieces accumulated in his palm, far more than her small offering warranted. "Sir, that's too much—"

"It's not nearly enough." Daniel pressed the coins into her trembling hand, his fingers warm against her cold skin. "Your father was a good man," he said, his voice steady but laced with emotion that made her chest tighten. "The best man I ever knew. You should not be living like this."

The coins felt like a lifeline in Holly's palm, each piece warm with promise and hope. She clutched them close, fighting back the tears that threatened to spill over completely. In the space of a few moments, this young man had reminded her of who she used to be—not just a servant girl selling scraps, but Holly Clarke, daughter of Reverend Thomas Clarke, worthy of kindness and remembrance.

"Thank you," she managed, her voice thick with gratitude that encompassed far more than the generous payment.

Daniel's gaze swept over her face with careful attention, as if memorising every detail after years of wondering what had become of the little girl who used to climb apple trees. "Holly, what happened? After your parents ..." He paused, struggling to find words that wouldn't deepen her obvious pain. "Where have you been living?"

"With my aunt. At Hart House." Holly's fingers tightened around the coins, their weight anchoring her to this moment of unexpected kindness. "She took me in when the village ladies wrote to her."

Something shifted in Daniel's expression—a hardening that transformed his gentle features into something more calculating. "Hart House," he repeated slowly, as if filing the information away. "And how does she treat you?"

Holly opened her mouth to offer the expected pleasantries, the careful lies Cordelia had trained into her. But looking into Daniel's eyes—eyes that remembered her father's goodness, that saw her as more than a burden—the truth tumbled out before she could stop it.

"She makes me work. In the kitchens, the floors. I sleep in the servants' quarters." The words felt dangerous on her tongue, but liberating. "She says I must earn my keep."

Daniel's jaw tightened. "Your father saved Mrs Bates from that fire. He gave his life for another's. Any daughter of Thomas Clarke deserves better than—"

The distant chime of the church bell cut through his words, and Daniel's eyes widened with sudden realisation. "I'm... I'm late for my tutorial." He glanced toward a street to their right, then back at Holly with obvious reluctance. "I'm studying so that I can go to Cambridge, to study law. I have class that I ..." He trailed off guiltily.

"You should go," Holly said softly, though every fibre of her being wanted him to stay, to keep talking, to remind her that she had once been someone worth remembering.

"Holly." Daniel reached out as if to touch her hand, then caught himself. "I hope to see you again soon. Very soon."

He stepped backward into the crowd, his dark coat swallowing the distance between them. Holly watched until he disappeared entirely, swallowed by the market's chaos. Only then did she look down at the coins in her palm, their silver surfaces catching the afternoon light.

For the first time in months, maybe years, warmth bloomed in her chest—not the desperate heat of fear, but something altogether different. Something that felt dangerously like hope.

Tonight, at least, Cordelia's wrath would find no purchase.

A PRESSING ISSUE

*D*aniel burst through the front doors of Thornhill Manor with uncharacteristic haste, his academic composure entirely forgotten. He found his father in the library, bent over correspondence at his mahogany desk, spectacles perched on his nose as he reviewed magistrate business.

"Father." Daniel's voice carried an urgency that made Sir Richard look up immediately. "I need to speak with you about something most pressing."

Sir Richard set down his pen, studying his son's agitated state. "What troubles you?"

"Holly Clarke." Daniel moved closer to the desk, his hands clenched at his sides. "Do you remember her? Reverend Clarke's daughter?"

"Of course. Sweet child. Terrible business about her parents." Sir Richard's expression softened with memory. "I heard the village ladies arranged for her to live with family here, in the city."

"Yes, with Lady Cordelia Hart." Daniel's tone turned sharp. "I encountered Holly in the market today, selling eggs for her aunt."

Sir Richard's eyebrows rose. "Selling eggs?"

"Father, you wouldn't recognise her." Daniel began pacing, his agitation spilling into movement. "She's thin as a reed, dressed in rags, working as if she were a common servant. This is the daughter of Thomas Clarke—the man who died saving Mrs Bates from that fire."

The magistrate's expression darkened. "What exactly did she tell you?"

"That her aunt makes her work—kitchens, floors, the lot. She sleeps in the servants' quarters." Daniel's voice cracked with indignation. "She's been reduced to hawking produce in the market square like a beggar child."

Sir Richard removed his spectacles, cleaning them with deliberate precision—a habit Daniel recognised as his father's way of controlling rising anger. "Lady Cordelia Hart, you said?"

"The very same."

"I know of her." Sir Richard's voice carried the measured tone he used in magistrate proceedings. "Married to Sir Geoffrey Hart. They move in society circles, though there have been ... whispers about their finances."

Daniel stopped pacing. "What sort of whispers?"

"Gambling debts. Drinking debts. Poor investments. The kind of troubles that might make a family view an orphaned heiress as either burden or opportunity." Sir Richard stood, his tall frame radiating authority. "This cannot stand, Daniel. Thomas Clarke was a man of uncommon virtue. His daughter deserves protection, not exploitation."

"What will you do?"

Sir Richard's jaw set with determination. "Tomorrow, I shall pay a call on Hart House. As a magistrate and as one who respected her father, I have every right to inquire after young Holly's welfare."

"And if you find what I suspect?"

"Then Lady Cordelia Hart will discover that justice extends beyond her drawing room."

RICHARD'S INQUIRY

Sir Richard approached Hart House the following afternoon, his magistrate's instincts already sharpened by Daniel's disturbing account. The imposing three-storey mansion loomed before him, its Georgian facade meticulously maintained despite whispers of the family's financial troubles. He pulled the brass bell with measured authority.

The butler who answered bore the polished demeanour of a household striving to maintain appearances. "Sir Richard Thornhill to see Lady Cordelia Hart," he announced, presenting his calling card.

Within moments, Lady Cordelia herself appeared in the entrance hall, her hands fluttering to her throat in what appeared to be genuine surprise. "Sir Richard! What an unexpected honour." Her voice carried the precise modulation of society breeding, yet something in her tone struck him as rehearsed.

"Lady Hart." He inclined his head respectfully. "I hope you'll forgive the unannounced visit. I've come to inquire after young Holly Clarke—Reverend Clarke's daughter. I understand she resides with you now."

Cordelia's composure wavered for the briefest moment before she dabbed her eyes with a delicate handkerchief. "Oh, Sir Richard, you're so kind to concern yourself with our dear Holly." Her voice trembled with what seemed like barely controlled emotion. "Please, do come in. Such a tragic affair— losing both parents so young."

She led him through corridors lined with family portraits and expensive furnishings, her movements graceful despite the weight of apparent sorrow. The drawing room she ushered him into bore all the marks of wealth—silk wallpaper, crystal decanters, furniture that spoke of generations of prosperity.

"Tea, Sir Richard?" Cordelia settled herself across from him, her black dress rustling softly. "I must apologise for the state of things. Caring for a grieving child whilst managing our own ... difficulties ... has proven rather overwhelming."

Sir Richard accepted the offered tea, studying his hostess carefully. "I trust Holly has adjusted well to her new circumstances? After all, it has been over three years now."

"As well as can be expected." Cordelia's sigh carried theatrical weight. "The poor child has been quite ... challenging since the tragedy. Grief manifests differently in the young, you understand. Some days she refuses to leave her room entirely."

"I see." Sir Richard set down his cup with deliberate precision. "And her education? Her father placed great importance on learning."

"Oh, we've arranged for tutoring, naturally." Cordelia waved her hand vaguely. "Though Holly has shown little interest in lessons. She seems to prefer ... simpler occupations. Helping with household tasks appears to comfort her."

Sir Richard's jaw tightened almost imperceptibly. The image of Holly selling eggs in the market square hardly suggested voluntary domestic comfort. "Might I see her? I knew her parents well, and I believe she might remember me."

Cordelia's eyes widened with apparent distress. "Oh, Sir

Richard, I'm afraid that's quite impossible today. Holly has been ... confined to her room for misbehaviour. She struck one of the servants this morning in a fit of temper. Such outbursts have become distressingly common."

"Indeed." The magistrate's voice remained carefully neutral, though every instinct screamed that something lay fundamentally wrong beneath Cordelia's performance.

"You cannot imagine the burden, Sir Richard." Cordelia's voice broke convincingly. "Geoffrey and I took her in without hesitation—family obligation, you understand—but our own circumstances have become rather ... strained. The costs of maintaining Hart House, coupled with caring for a troubled child ..." She gestured helplessly around the opulent room.

Every word felt calculated, yet Sir Richard found himself without concrete evidence to challenge her claims. The woman before him presented every appearance of a long-suffering relative overwhelmed by unexpected responsibilities.

"Perhaps," he suggested carefully, "there are village families who might assist? Holly grew up among them, after all."

"Charity?" Cordelia's voice sharpened before she caught herself. "Sir Richard, surely you understand that we cannot subject a child of good family to the uncertainties of village charity. Whatever her ... difficulties ... Holly deserves the stability only proper family can provide."

Sir Richard rose, his visit yielding nothing but deeper unease. "Of course. Please give Holly my regards when she's ... available."

"Certainly." Cordelia accompanied him to the door, her performance never wavering. "Your concern touches me deeply, Sir Richard. It's comforting to know that Thomas Clarke's friends remember his family with such kindness."

Standing on Hart House's steps moments later, Sir Richard felt the weight of frustration settling in his chest. Cordelia's tears, her explanations, her apparent sacrifice—all perfectly reasonable on the surface. Yet every magistrate's instinct he possessed whispered of deception beneath the polished veneer.

Without evidence, without witnessing actual wrongdoing, his hands remained tied. But Daniel's account of the girl in the market square haunted him. Somewhere within that grand house, Holly Clarke was either a troubled child receiving necessary discipline, or a victim of circumstances far darker than Cordelia's performance suggested.

He would be watching. And waiting.

SOLUTIONS

$\mathcal{T}$he front door closed with a satisfying thud, but Cordelia's composure cracked the moment Sir Richard's footsteps faded down the front sidewalk. Her fingers trembled as she pressed them against the polished mahogany, rage coursing through her veins like poison.

"That interfering magistrate," she hissed through clenched teeth. The drawing room's opulent furnishings suddenly felt suffocating, witnesses to her performance that had cost her dearly to maintain.

She swept through the corridors, her silk skirt rustling against the Persian runners. Gas lamps cast dancing shadows on the ancestral portraits, their painted eyes seeming to follow her agitated movement. Each step echoed her mounting fury—fury at Holly's very existence, at the inheritance that rightfully belonged to her, at the complications this wretched child continued to create.

"Geoffrey!" Her voice rang through the house with imperial authority.

She found him in his study, naturally, slumped in his leather chair with a crystal tumbler balanced precariously in his lap.

The brandy had already begun its familiar work, dulling his conscience and rendering him pliable to her will.

"Sir Richard Thornhill paid us a visit," she announced, watching Geoffrey's bleary eyes struggle to focus. "Asking questions about our dear niece."

Geoffrey's hand tightened around his glass. "Questions?"

"The kind of questions magistrates ask when they suspect something amiss." Cordelia began pacing the study's length, her mind working with calculating precision. "Holly has been talking, Geoffrey. Spreading tales of her treatment here."

"Perhaps we should—"

"Should what?" Her voice cut through his stammering like a blade. "Send her back to those village idiots? Let her inherit Roseworth and leave us to rot in debtor's prison?"

The room fell silent except for the steady tick of the mantel clock. Cordelia paused before the window, staring out at the grounds that might soon slip through their fingers if Holly lived to claim her inheritance.

"That child brings nothing but trouble," she muttered, her reflection ghostlike in the darkening glass. Her mind churned with possibilities, each more ruthless than the last. Accidents had failed. Neglect had only made the girl stronger. But there were other ways—permanent ways—to solve troublesome problems.

Geoffrey's glass clinked against the side table as he reached for the decanter again, seeking oblivion from whatever darkness his wife was conjuring. But Cordelia barely noticed his retreat into drink. Her thoughts had turned to solutions that would require neither loose stones nor fraying ropes.

Solutions that would ensure Holly Clarke never lived to see her twenty-first birthday.

DINNER

The dining room felt different that evening. Holly couldn't place what had changed—perhaps the way the candlelight flickered across the mahogany table, casting shadows that seemed to reach toward her with grasping fingers. The crystal glasses caught the flame and threw fragments of light against the wallpaper, creating an almost festive atmosphere that felt entirely at odds with the oppressive silence.

Cordelia had outdone herself with the table setting. The finest china gleamed beneath the chandelier, each piece positioned with mathematical precision. Silver cutlery flanked Holly's plate like sentries, and a small bouquet of hothouse flowers dominated the centre of the table—an unusual touch of beauty that made Holly's chest ache with memories of her mother's garden.

"Sit," Cordelia commanded, gesturing to the chair with an elaborate flourish.

Holly lowered herself onto the velvet cushion, her hands folding automatically in her lap. The familiar routine of evening prayers felt impossible here, beneath Cordelia's watchful gaze.

Instead, she stared at the bowl before her—a rich lamb stew that steamed invitingly in the warm air.

The aroma should have made her mouth water. After weeks of meagre portions and cold leftovers eaten in the servants' quarters, the sight of proper food should have been a blessing. Yet something twisted in her stomach, a warning she couldn't name.

"Eat," Cordelia said, settling into her own chair with feline grace. "You're far too thin, child. People will think I'm not feeding you properly."

Holly lifted the spoon with trembling fingers. The silver felt impossibly heavy, as though weighted with lead. She stirred the stew, watching carrots and potatoes surface and disappear in the rich brown gravy. It looked exactly like the meals Cook used to prepare at Roseworth—hearty, warming food that spoke of care and nourishment.

But this wasn't Roseworth, and these weren't loving hands that had prepared it.

"I'm not terribly hungry," Holly whispered, setting the spoon aside.

Cordelia's eyes flashed with something dangerous. "Not hungry? After all the trouble I've taken to provide you with a proper meal?"

Holly forced herself to lift the spoon again, bringing a small portion toward her lips. The smell hit her nostrils—rich meat, herbs, something else she couldn't identify. Something that made her pause.

"What's wrong with you?" Cordelia's voice grew sharp, cutting through the flickering candlelight. "Are you so ungrateful that you'll turn your nose up at good food?"

"I just—" Holly began, but Cordelia's chair scraped against the floor as she stood abruptly.

"Eat that stew this instant, or you'll have nothing for a week."

Holly's spoon hovered over the bowl. The steam rose in delicate spirals, carrying that strange, medicinal undertone that made her stomach churn. She thought of her mother's gentle hands ladling soup into wooden bowls, of her father's blessing over their simple meals. This felt nothing like those moments of grace.

Cordelia's patience snapped like a taut wire. "Fine. Starve then, you wretched creature."

She swept from the room in a rustle of silk, leaving Holly alone with the untouched stew and the oppressive weight of the shadows. The candles continued their restless dance, and Holly found herself staring at the bowl as though it might reveal its secrets.

Footsteps approached from the corridor—lighter than Cordelia's imperious stride. Mrs Dawes appeared in the doorway, her weathered face creased with concern.

"Miss Holly?" The cook's voice carried a tremor Holly had never heard before. "You haven't touched your dinner."

"I'm not very hungry, Mrs Dawes."

The older woman stepped closer, her eyes fixed on the bowl with growing alarm. "Child, step away from that table. Now."

Something in Mrs Dawes's tone sent ice through Holly's veins. She pushed back from the table, the chair legs scraping against the floor.

"I saw her," Mrs Dawes whispered. The cook's hands shook as she pointed at the stew. ""Lady Cordelia ... I watched her add something to your bowl—laudanum from the medicine cabinet. Enough to ..."

Holly's breath caught in her throat. The spoon clattered from her nerveless fingers onto the fine china, the sound echoing through the dining room like a death knell.

Before either of them could move, a sleek shadow darted between their feet. Cordelia's prized Persian cat had slipped into the room, drawn by the rich aroma of meat. The creature leaped onto the table with feline grace, its whiskers twitching as it investigated the abandoned feast.

"No!" Holly lunged forward, but too late.

The cat's pink tongue lapped at the poisoned gravy, its purr rumbling with satisfaction at this unexpected treat. For a moment, nothing happened. The animal continued eating, delicate paws balanced on the table's edge.

Then the convulsions began.

The cat's body arched unnaturally, its spine contorting as violent spasms seized its limbs. A horrible yowling filled the dining room—a sound of pure agony that seemed to echo from the very walls of Hart House. The creature's eyes rolled back, showing only white, as foam gathered at its mouth.

Holly pressed her hands to her ears, but nothing could block out the cat's death throes. The animal thrashed on the mahogany table, knocking over crystal glasses and scattering the carefully arranged flowers. China shattered against the floor in a symphony of destruction.

Mrs Dawes grabbed Holly's shoulders, pulling her back from the horrible scene. "Don't look, child. Don't look."

But Holly couldn't tear her gaze away. The cat's suffering continued for what felt like hours but could only have been minutes. Finally, mercifully, the creature went still, its body twisted in a final, desperate arch.

The dining room fell silent except for Holly's ragged breathing and the steady drip of spilled wine from the overturned glasses. The cat lay motionless among the ruins of Cordelia's elegant table setting, a testament to the poison that had been meant for Holly's lips.

Mrs Dawes's voice cut through the silence, barely a whisper: "She meant to kill you, child. God help us all, she meant to kill you."

BREAD CRUMBS & BORROWED FAITH

*T*he clock in the entrance hall chimed midnight, but Holly remained wide awake in her cramped servant's room, staring at the ceiling whilst the cat's death throes replayed endlessly behind her closed eyelids. Each time she tried to push the images away, they returned with fresh horror —the arched spine, the foam at its mouth, the terrible yowling that had filled the dining room like a banshee's wail.

That could have been her. Should have been her.

Holly's heart hammered against her ribs as the full weight of understanding settled upon her chest like a gravestone. Cordelia hadn't simply been cruel or indifferent—she had tried to murder her own niece. The accidents, the loose stone, the frayed rope—none of it had been coincidence. Her aunt wanted her dead. It was certain.

A scream pierced the night silence, echoing through Hart House's corridors with raw anguish. Cordelia had discovered her precious Persian cat amongst the ruins of the dining room. Holly pressed her hands to her mouth, stifling the sob that threatened to escape as she listened to her aunt's cries of grief and rage.

But beneath Cordelia's theatrical mourning, Holly detected something else—fury at a failed plan, not genuine sorrow for a beloved pet. The cat had been an inconvenience, nothing more. A witness to attempted murder that could never testify.

Another scream reverberated through the walls, followed by Geoffrey's stammering attempts at comfort. Holly heard footsteps pacing the floor above, Cordelia's voice rising and falling in what sounded like accusations. How long before her aunt realised what had truly happened? How long before she decided to try again?

Holly's survival instinct blazed to life, sending adrenaline coursing through her veins. She couldn't stay here another moment. Not another hour. Cordelia would find another way—something less obvious than poison, perhaps. An accident that left no evidence, no witnesses save a grief-stricken aunt mourning her tragic loss.

With trembling fingers, Holly reached beneath her thin mattress and retrieved the heel of bread she'd hidden there—a pathetic provision, but all she possessed. Her Bible lay beside it, Mrs Dawes's precious gift wrapped in a scrap of cloth. Holly clutched both to her chest, feeling their solid weight against her racing heart.

The floorboards above creaked ominously as heavy footsteps moved back and forth. Cordelia's voice carried through the walls, sharp and dangerous. Holly didn't dare light a candle to gather more belongings. Every second she remained in Hart House brought her closer to death.

She slipped from beneath her threadbare blanket, bare feet touching the cold stone floor. The servant's corridor stretched before her like a tunnel to freedom or a passage to hell—she couldn't be sure which. Each step seemed to echo despite her careful movements, every creak of the ancient floorboards amplifying her heartbeat until she was certain the entire house could hear her escape.

The back door loomed ahead, its iron handle gleaming faintly in the darkness. Holly's hand closed around the cold metal, and she turned it with infinite care. The hinges protested with a soft groan that made her freeze, listening for any sign that she'd been discovered.

Silence.

Cold night air rushed against her face as the door swung open, carrying the scent of frost and freedom. Holly stepped into the shadows of Hart House's rear garden, feeling the cobblestones beneath her shoes like stepping stones across a treacherous river. The roses she'd tended still climbed the wall, their thorns catching the faint moonlight like tiny daggers.

She ran.

Her feet barely whispered against the stones as she fled through Ashford's sleeping streets, driven by pure terror. Gas lamps cast pools of yellow light that she darted between like a ghost, avoiding the illuminated circles where someone might spot a fleeing child. The market district lay ahead—a maze of narrow alleys and shadowed doorways where she might disappear.

Holly's lungs burned as she pressed deeper into the labyrinth of back streets. Her thin, worn dress caught on rough brick walls, tearing in places, but she didn't slow her desperate flight. Behind her, Hart House sat in darkness, its windows like dead eyes watching her escape.

When exhaustion finally overwhelmed her, Holly found herself in a narrow alley wedged between two towering buildings. The space reeked of rotting vegetables and worse things she didn't want to identify. Her legs gave out, and she collapsed against the grimy brick wall, gasping for breath that misted white in the frigid air.

The alley felt like a tomb—dirt, shadows, and uncertainty pressing in from all sides. Yet it was safer than the gilded cage of

Hart House, where death had worn silk gowns and spoken in refined tones. Here, at least, the dangers were honest.

A street lamp flickered at the alley's mouth, casting wavering light across the refuse scattered on the ground. Holly pressed the bread against her chest, feeling its meagre comfort as tears began to stream down her cheeks. The hunger that had gnawed at her for months now felt like a living thing, clawing at her empty stomach with renewed savagery.

She thought of her mother's gentle hands breaking bread at their cottage table, of grace spoken over simple meals that had tasted like love itself. Those memories felt like glimpses of another world—a place of warmth and safety that might have been a dream for all its distance from this cold alley.

Holly pulled her Bible from its cloth wrapping, holding it close as sobs shook her thin shoulders. The leather cover felt warm against her skin.

"Please," she whispered into the darkness, her voice barely audible above the distant sounds of the sleeping city. "Mother said you see even the sparrows fall. Please see me now."

The words her mother had spoken in the rose garden came back to her like an echo: "Even in ashes, they bloom again." But Holly felt like nothing more than ash herself—scattered and broken, with no hope of blooming anywhere.

She clutched the Bible tighter, pressing her face against its worn cover as tears fell freely. Somewhere in the distance, a church bell tolled the hour, its bronze voice carrying across the rooftops like a prayer made manifest.

Holly closed her eyes and listened to its fading echo, wondering if this was how her story would end—alone in an alley with nothing but bread crumbs and borrowed faith to sustain her through the long, cold night ahead.

WAITING FOR DAWN

*T*he hours crawled past like wounded animals, each minute stretching into an eternity of cold and uncertainty. Holly pressed herself deeper into the alley's darkest corner, where the brick walls met in a protective embrace that shielded her from the wind but not from her racing thoughts.

Every sound made her heart leap—the scurry of rats across cobblestones, the distant clatter of a late carriage, the mournful cry of a cat somewhere in the labyrinth of streets. Each noise might herald discovery, might bring Cordelia's servants hunting through the alleys with lanterns and cruel intentions.

The hunger had grown beyond mere discomfort now. It twisted through her belly like a living serpent, sharp and insistent, making her light-headed despite her desperate need to stay alert. The small heel of bread felt precious as gold in her hands, but she dared not eat more than the tiniest crumbs. This might be all the food she would have for days.

Holly's mind churned with impossible choices. Return to Hart House and face whatever new horrors Cordelia had devised? The woman had already tried to poison her—what fresh torments awaited if Holly crawled back like a beaten dog?

The thought of Cordelia's cold blue eyes gleaming with triumph made her stomach clench with something beyond hunger.

But what alternative existed? A thirteen-year-old girl alone on the streets with nothing but a thin worn dress, a bag with her mother's old blue dress, and a handful of bread crumbs stood little chance against the harsh realities of city life. She'd heard whispered stories of what befell children who disappeared into Ashford's darker quarters—tales that made even the adults cross themselves and hurry past certain districts after sunset.

The shadows seemed to shift and writhe in her peripheral vision, playing tricks born of exhaustion and fear. Sometimes she glimpsed figures moving in the darkness, only to realise they were merely her own terror given shape by moonlight and desperation.

Yet beneath the fear, something else began to stir. A tiny flame of defiance that refused to be extinguished, fed by memories of her father's courage and her mother's final words. The roses at Roseworth had survived neglect and harsh winters. They endured because survival was written into their very nature.

Holly pressed her face against the Bible's worn leather cover, drawing strength from its familiar weight. "Even in ashes, they bloom again," she whispered into the darkness, tasting the truth of those words for the first time since her mother had spoken them.

She would not return to Hart House. Whatever lay ahead in these unknown streets, it could not be worse than the gilded cage where death wore silk and spoke in honeyed tones. Here, at least, the dangers would be honest—born of desperation rather than calculated malice.

The decision settled into her bones like warmth returning to frozen limbs. She would forge her own path, however treacherous, rather than surrender to Cordelia's schemes. The inheritance, Roseworth, even her own safety—all of it mattered less than this moment of choosing her own destiny.

Dawn crept across the sky like spilled watercolours, painting the alley mouth in shades of grey and gold. The first tentative light touched Holly's upturned face as she rose to her feet, clutching the bread, bag and Bible against her chest like talismans.

Her legs trembled from cold and exhaustion, but her spirit felt steadier than it had in months. The unknown stretched before her like an unmarked map, full of perils she couldn't imagine but also possibilities she dared not hope for.

Holly stepped toward the alley's mouth, where morning light beckoned with promises she couldn't yet understand. Her next steps remained uncertain, but they would be her own.

STREET WISDOM

The morning burst alive around Holly as she emerged from the alley's mouth into the chaos of market day. Voices rose in a symphony of haggling and hawking, cart wheels rattled across uneven cobblestones, and the scents of fresh bread and ripe fruit mingled with less pleasant odours from the gutters. The assault on her senses made her stumble, over-whelmed after the long hours of silent darkness.

Children's laughter pierced through the cacophony like silver bells, drawing her gaze to a group of young ones weaving between the market stalls with practised ease. Their joy seemed impossible in such surroundings—genuine delight rising from the very streets that had terrified her through the night. The sound tugged at something deep within her chest, a painful reminder of games played in Ashford Green when the world had been safe and predictable.

Holly pressed herself against a shop wall, watching the organised chaos unfold before her. Vendors called their wares whilst customers examined goods with suspicious eyes. Pick-pockets moved like shadows through the crowd. Women clutched their purses closer whilst men kept hands on their watch chains. Yet through it all, the children played their games of survival with a lightness that spoke of resilience beyond their years.

A group of street children had gathered near an abandoned stall, their animated voices carrying above the market din. Holly found herself drawn toward them despite her better judgement, something in their easy camaraderie calling to the loneliness that had become her constant companion at Hart House.

"Right then, who's brave enough to try the apple trick again?" called out a girl with wild dark hair and dirt-smudged cheeks. Her grin blazed with mischief as she held up a wrinkled apple, tossing it from hand to hand with careless confidence. "Tom nearly got us caught yesterday, so we need someone with proper fingers for this."

The girl's eyes swept across her companions before landing on Holly, who stood frozen at the edge of their circle. Something shifted in the girl's expression—recognition, perhaps, or simply the acknowledgement of fresh prey.

"Well, well." The girl sauntered over with the swagger of someone who owned the streets beneath her feet. "What have we here? You look like a bird that fell from its nest!"

Holly's cheeks burned with embarrassment and fear, but before she could retreat, the girl had grasped her elbow with surprising gentleness.

"I'm Nell," she announced, as if that explained everything. "And you, little bird, look like you could use some proper friends. Come on then—no point standing about like a lost lamb when the wolves are prowling."

The warmth in Nell's voice contrasted sharply with her rough appearance. Her dress was a patchwork of mismatched fabrics held together with stubborn hope and careful stitching. Yet she carried herself with the confidence of a duchess, unbowed by circumstances that would have crushed lesser spirits.

"These streets will eat you alive if you don't know the rules," Nell continued, steering Holly toward the group with practised ease. "Lucky for you, I happen to be the finest teacher of street wisdom from here to London."

Holly allowed herself to be drawn into the circle, her Bible clutched against her chest like armour. The other children assessed her with curious but not unkind eyes—calculating her worth as ally or burden in the unforgiving arithmetic of survival.

"First lesson," Nell announced with theatrical flair, "is knowing your friends from your enemies. See that constable over there? The one with the brass buttons trying to look important? He's got wandering hands and a taste for tossing kids into the workhouse for sport. Avoid him like the plague."

Holly followed Nell's gaze to a pompous-looking officer who was indeed eyeing their group with suspicious interest. Her stomach clenched at the thought of official attention—what if Cordelia had already reported her missing? What if there were people looking for her even now?

"Don't look so terrified, little bird." Nell's laugh bubbled up like water from a spring. "We've all got our stories of woe. The trick is not letting them drag you under."

As Nell chattered on about the unwritten laws of street life— which doorways offered shelter, which shopkeepers might spare a crust, how to vanish when the workhouse gangs came prowling—Holly found herself oddly comforted. Here was someone who understood that survival required more than just hope and prayers.

"And that quiet fellow over there," Nell gestured toward a figure sitting apart from the main group, "is Benjamin. Don't let his shy nature fool you—he's got the cleverest hands in all of Ashford."

Holly turned to see a young man of perhaps seventeen years, his dark hair falling across his forehead as he worked with intense concentration. His fingers moved with surprising dexterity as he wove scraps of rope and discarded paper into a small but sturdy basket. When he noticed her attention, he looked up with eyes the colour of warm chocolate.

"Another new friend, Nell?" Benjamin's voice carried a gentle Welsh lilt that reminded Holly painfully of her father's reading voice. Despite sitting on the ground, she could see he favoured one leg over the other—his left foot turned inward at an unnatural angle.

"This one's special," Nell declared with the authority of someone who'd made such pronouncements before. "Got that look about her—like she's seen too much but hasn't given up hope yet."

Benjamin set aside his weaving and studied Holly with quiet intensity. When he smiled, it transformed his entire face, chasing away the shadows that seemed to cling to all of them.

"We all have our challenges," he said simply, gesturing to his twisted foot without shame or self-pity. "Can't let a little thing like a clubfoot keep me from making a living. These hands work just fine, and there's always someone willing to pay for a proper basket or a clean crossing."

His matter-of-fact acceptance of his circumstances struck Holly with unexpected force. Here was someone who'd found purpose despite—or perhaps because of—the obstacles life had placed in his path. No bitter resentment, no rage at unfair fortune, just quiet determination to make the best of what he'd been given.

"Benjamin makes the prettiest flower arrangements you ever saw," Nell added with obvious pride. "Turns the ugliest weeds into something fit for a lady's parlour. Real artist, he is."

The praise brought colour to Benjamin's cheeks, but he didn't dispute it. Instead, he reached into his basket and withdrew a small posy of wildflowers—dandelions and clover woven together with surprising skill. He offered it to Holly with the same ceremony another might present a diamond bracelet.

"Welcome to our little family," he said softly. "Such as it is."

Holly accepted the flowers with trembling fingers, overwhelmed by this simple act of kindness from someone who had even less than she did. For the first time since fleeing Hart House, she felt something other than fear or desperation.

She felt hope.

FINDING PURPOSE

*U*nder Nell's watchful eye, Holly crouched beside a patch of wild forget-me-nots that had pushed through the cobblestones near the market's edge. Her fingers moved with growing confidence as she selected the finest stems, remembering her mother's lessons about choosing flowers at their peak.

"Not those ones," Nell instructed, pointing to a cluster with browning edges. "Customers won't pay good coin for wilted blooms. You want the ones that look like they just opened to greet the morning sun."

Holly nodded, adjusting her selection. The knowledge felt familiar beneath her fingertips—the way to test a stem's firmness, how to judge which flowers would last longest once cut. Her mother's voice seemed to whisper through her hands as she worked.

"Now watch how Benjamin arranges them," Nell continued, settling beside them on the damp ground. "He's got an eye for making magic from scraps."

Benjamin's twisted foot didn't hinder his grace as he worked. Holly observed how he balanced colours and textures, creating small bouquets that seemed to capture sunlight itself. His damaged limb simply became part of his rhythm as he shifted his weight, concentrating entirely on the flowers before him.

"The secret," Benjamin explained, weaving a strand of wild grass through the forget-me-nots, "is telling a story with each arrangement. This one speaks of faithfulness and remembrance —perfect for a gentleman caller or someone visiting a grave."

Holly attempted to copy his technique, her first efforts clumsy but earnest. The forget-me-nots resisted her inexperienced fingers, stems snapping or petals falling loose. Frustration bubbled up, but Benjamin's patient encouragement kept her working.

"Better already," he murmured as Holly produced a passable small posy. "Now comes the harder part—convincing strangers to part with their coins."

The prospect of approaching customers sent anxiety crawling up Holly's spine. She'd grown used to invisibility at Hart House, to moving through the world without drawing attention. The thought of deliberately seeking notice felt like stepping naked into the marketplace.

"Start with the kind-looking ones," Nell advised, scanning the crowd for suitable targets. "That woman there, with the gentle smile—she'll not bite your head off even if she doesn't buy."

Holly approached the woman with trembling steps, her small bouquet held before her like a shield. The words caught in her throat as curious eyes turned her way.

"Fresh flowers, ma'am?" she managed, her voice barely above a whisper.

The woman paused, studying Holly's handiwork with genuine interest. "Oh, how lovely! Such a sweet arrangement. Did you make this yourself, dear?"

Holly nodded, unable to find more words. But the woman's smile grew warmer as she examined the flowers more closely.

"Beautiful work. Here's tuppence for your troubles." The coins clinked into Holly's palm like tiny miracles. "You've quite the talent for this."

The compliment blazed through Holly's chest, kindling something she'd thought lost forever. Purpose. Worth. The knowledge that her hands could create something others valued.

As the day wore on, Holly's confidence grew with each successful sale. Her voice strengthened, her posture straightened. The shy whisper became a clear offer, her arrangements improved with practice. When evening fell, she'd earned enough coins to buy bread for herself and her new companions.

But the nights proved crueller than the days. Holly huddled in a doorway between Nell and Benjamin, the three of them pressed together for warmth as wind whistled through the narrow alley. Her thin dress, once fine enough for Hart House servants, provided little protection against the autumn chill that crept through every gap in the buildings.

Sleep came in fragments between shivers. Holly's stomach cramped with hunger despite the bread they'd shared—a few mouthfuls that only reminded her body of its constant need. She dreamed of her mother's warm kitchen, of thick stews and fresh bread, of fires that chased away every shadow.

Dawn brought new misery. Holly's muscles ached from sleeping on stone, her bones stiff with cold. Benjamin stirred first, stretching his good leg carefully before attempting to stand. The simple act of rising seemed to require tremendous effort.

"Gets easier," he said quietly, catching Holly's expression. "Your body learns to expect less comfort."

But even as hunger gnawed at her belly and cold settled into her bones, Holly discovered unexpected compensation. Around the small fires they built in hidden corners, stories flowed like wine. Nell regaled them with tales of her adventures—narrow escapes from constables, kindnesses from unexpected strangers, the strange characters who populated the city's forgotten corners.

Benjamin shared quieter stories, memories of his Welsh valley home before circumstances drove him to the streets. His voice carried the rhythm of distant mountains as he spoke of sheep bells and morning mist.

And Holly found herself talking too, sharing memories of Roseworth's garden, of her father's gentle sermons, of her mother's music. The words emerged hesitantly at first, then with growing confidence as she saw how her companions listened without judgment.

Other children began joining their circle as word spread of the flower girl who told stories. Street children who couldn't read, orphans who'd forgotten their own names, lost souls seeking something beyond mere survival. Holly retrieved her hidden Bible, its worn pages soft beneath her fingers.

"This one's about a mustard seed," she began one evening, the firelight dancing across young faces. "How something tiny can grow into something magnificent if it's planted in good soil."

The children leaned closer, hungry for hope as much as bread. Holly's voice grew stronger as she read, remembering her father's gift for making scripture come alive. She spoke of David facing giants, of Daniel surviving lions, of ordinary people finding extraordinary courage when faith filled their hearts.

Laughter began mixing with their tears. Dreams crept back into conversations once devoted only to survival. And Holly discovered that in nurturing others' hopes, her own began to take root again—fragile but growing, like her mother's roses pushing through winter soil.

FIGHTING TOGETHER

*T*he afternoon sun cast long shadows across the market square as Holly arranged her latest bouquet—daisies and wild rosemary she'd gathered from the commons, at dawn. Her fingers moved with practiced ease now, weaving stems into pleasing patterns that caught the light. The past weeks had sharpened her skills, each day teaching her something new about colour, texture, the art of making beauty from scraps.

"Mind the gentleman with the walking stick," Nell murmured, nodding toward a well-dressed man examining Benjamin's baskets. "He's been watching us for ten minutes."

Holly's stomach tightened. She'd learned to read the signs—the way certain people studied them with calculating eyes, the difference between customers and those with darker purposes. The gentleman moved on, but unease lingered like smoke in the air.

"Fresh flowers!" Holly called, her voice carrying across the cobblestones. "Bright posies for your tables!"

A woman in a blue bonnet approached, admiring Holly's handiwork. As they negotiated the price, Holly caught sight of uniformed figures moving through the crowd. Her blood chilled. Workhouse officials, their grey coats unmistakable even at a distance, working methodically through the market stalls.

Nell's sharp intake of breath confirmed Holly's fears. The older girl's hand shot out, gripping Holly's wrist with sudden urgency.

"Now," Nell hissed. "Drop everything. Move."

Holly's flowers scattered across the cobblestones as Nell pulled her behind a fishmonger's cart. Benjamin followed, his uneven gait made swift by desperation. They pressed against the wooden wheels, hearts hammering as boots clicked past mere inches away.

"Three children reported sleeping rough," one official said, his voice carrying clearly. "Young girl with auburn hair among them. Lady Hart's put up a reward for information."

Holly's breath caught. Cordelia hadn't forgotten. Hadn't forgiven. Even here, in this maze of strangers and shadows, her aunt's reach extended like poisonous tendrils.

"Check the flower sellers," another voice commanded. "Street children often gravitate to harmless occupations."

The boots moved closer. Holly could smell fish scales and salt, feel Nell's rapid breathing against her shoulder. Benjamin's face had gone pale, his dark eyes fixed on the gap between cart wheels where uniformed legs paced back and forth.

Fear crawled up Holly's throat like bile. The workhouse meant separation from Nell and Benjamin, meant scrubbing floors and eating gruel and never seeing sunlight except through barred windows. It meant returning to Hart House eventually, to Cordelia's cold smile and whatever fresh torments awaited.

But worse than her own terror was the knowledge that her presence endangered her friends. Benjamin's clubfoot made him easily identifiable. Nell's fierce loyalty would never let her abandon Holly to save herself. They would all suffer because of her.

The officials' voices grew fainter as they moved toward the centre of the square. Nell's grip loosened slightly, but her eyes remained alert, scanning for escape routes.

"They'll circle back," she whispered. "Always do."

Holly nodded, understanding flooding through her. This wasn't safety—it was temporary reprieve. The workhouse officials would return tomorrow, next week, as often as necessary until they found what they sought. And Cordelia's gold would ensure they kept looking.

The reality of street life pressed down like a weight. There was no true hiding, no permanent sanctuary. Only constant vigilance, endless movement, the exhausting dance of staying one step ahead of those who would cage them.

But as Benjamin's hand found hers in the shadows, as Nell's fierce protectiveness radiated through the small space, Holly felt something stronger than fear. They were not alone in this fight.

THE FLOWER GIRL WHO PRAYS

Four years had passed since Holly first fled into Ashford's unforgiving streets, and the frightened thirteen-year-old had bloomed into something remarkable. At seventeen, she moved through the market with quiet grace, her auburn hair catching the morning light like burnished copper. Beneath the patched dress and worn shawl, her beauty had emerged—not the artificial polish of drawing rooms, but something deeper, forged in hardship and tempered by faith.

Her green eyes held depths that spoke of suffering transformed into compassion, of a spirit that refused to break despite everything the world had thrown at her. When she smiled—and she did smile, often and genuinely—it lit her entire face, drawing people like moths to a flame.

"Fresh flowers!" Holly called, arranging her morning's collection on the worn blanket that served as her stall. "Bright blooms to chase away the gloom!"

An old woman shuffled forward, coins clutched in arthritic fingers. "Might I have some of those yellow ones, dear? For my Harold's grave."

Holly selected the finest daffodils, weaving them into a delicate posy with trailing ivy. "These will last days," she said softly, pressing the arrangement into weathered hands. "And Harold will know you're thinking of him."

The woman's eyes misted. "You're that flower girl, aren't you? The one who prays for folks?"

Holly's reputation had grown like wildfire through Ashford's poorest quarters. They called her "the flower girl who prays," and the name carried weight among those who had precious little else to cling to. Street sweepers would tip their caps when she passed. Beggars would save her the choicest spots near the cathedral steps. Children would run to her when hunger or fear overwhelmed them.

"I pray with folks," Holly corrected gently. "We all need someone to listen."

Then Holly pressed a penny into the old woman's palm and she hurried away, clutching her flowers like treasure.

"Still giving away half your earnings, I see," Nell observed, appearing at Holly's elbow with her characteristic grin. At twenty, Nell had grown into a striking young woman, her dark hair tamed into a practical braid, her clothing still patched but cleaner now. The fierce protectiveness remained, but four years of watching Holly work miracles had softened some of her harder edges.

"Mrs Patterson's pension barely covers bread," Holly replied, organising her remaining blooms. "What's a penny when it means Harold gets proper flowers?"

Nell shook her head in fond exasperation. They'd had this conversation countless times, but Holly's generosity never wavered. If anything, it had grown stronger as the years passed, expanding beyond flowers to encompass anyone who crossed her path in need.

Benjamin approached, leaning heavily on his broom after a morning's work at the crossings. The clubfoot that had once made him self-conscious now seemed irrelevant—his broad shoulders and steady presence commanded respect among the street children who looked to him for protection. Dark stubble shadowed his jaw, and his eyes held the quiet confidence of someone who'd found his place in the world, even if you worked hard for it.

"Evening service tonight?" he asked, settling beside them with a grunt of relief.

"Under the old bridge," Holly confirmed. "Young Jimmy's been asking about the loaves and fishes again."

Their makeshift prayer services had become legend in Ashford's forgotten corners. Every few evenings, Holly would gather whoever needed sanctuary—street children shivering in doorways, mothers scraping by on charity, old men with nowhere else to turn. They'd huddle together in abandoned buildings or beneath stone bridges, and Holly would speak of hope in a voice that somehow made it seem possible.

Tonight, seventeen souls gathered as shadows lengthened across the city. Holly lit a precious candle stub, its flame dancing in the damp air beneath the bridge's arch. Faces emerged from the gloom—some young, some ancient, all marked by hardship but softened by expectation.

"We light this candle for little Martha," Holly began, her voice carrying clearly through the space. "Taken by fever last week. May she rest in peace, and may her mother find comfort."

Murmured amens rippled through the group. This had become their ritual—acknowledging those lost to the streets, keeping their memories alive when no one else would. Holly reached into her pocket and withdrew another stub, lighting it from the first.

"For old Jenkins, who used to share his soup with anyone who asked. May his kindness inspire us all."

More candles followed. Each flame represented someone who'd mattered, someone whose life had touched theirs however briefly. The abandoned space transformed into something sacred, something that belonged to them alone.

Holly opened her worn Bible. "Tonight I want to tell you about a man who fed thousands with just a few loaves and fishes."

Jimmy, barely eight and perpetually hungry, leaned forward eagerly. He'd heard this story before, but it never lost its magic—the promise that small offerings could become something miraculous.

As Holly spoke, her voice weaving through the familiar tale, others began to join in. They knew these stories now, had heard them countless times around flickering candles and makeshift fires. But somehow, spoken in Holly's clear tones, they became new again—promises meant specifically for them.

"The disciples said it wasn't enough," Holly continued, her eyes moving from face to face. "Five loaves, two fishes, thousands of hungry people. Impossible odds. But they gave what they had anyway."

Benjamin nodded slowly. He understood. They all did. Every day was impossible odds—finding food, staying warm, avoiding the workhouse officials who still occasionally swept through looking for strays. But they kept offering what little they had, and somehow it multiplied.

Nell's voice rose to join Holly's as she recited the familiar ending: "And they all ate and were satisfied, and they took up twelve baskets full of the broken pieces left over."

A chorus of voices followed, street children and desperate adults united in words that promised abundance from poverty, hope from despair. The sound echoed off ancient stones, creating something beautiful from the forgotten corners of the world.

Later, as the group dispersed into the night, an old woman pressed a copper coin into Holly's hand. "For more candles, dear. We'll need them for next time."

Holly smiled, tucking the coin carefully away. Tomorrow she'd buy bread for Jimmy and still have enough for herself. Somehow, there was always enough.

As they walked back toward their usual shelter, Nell shook her head in wonder. "Almost four years I've watched you do this. Still don't understand how you manage it."

"Manage what?"

"Making miracles seem ordinary."

Holly laughed, linking arms with her dearest friend. "That's not me. That's just faith doing what it's meant to do—growing in the dark until it's strong enough to bloom."

Above them, stars wheeled through smoky skies, and somewhere in the distance, church bells chimed the hour. Tomorrow would bring new struggles, fresh hardships, but also new chances to plant seeds of hope in forgotten corners.

The flower girl who prayed walked on through Ashford's sleeping streets, carrying light wherever shadows gathered deepest.

RECOGNITION

*D*aniel Thornhill strode through Ashford's misty morning streets with the confident bearing of a man who had just achieved something remarkable. At twenty years old, he wore his newly acquired barrister's robes with quiet pride—black fabric that billowed slightly in the autumn breeze, marking him as qualified an entire year earlier than expected. His father's rigorous teachings and Daniel's own relentless dedication had propelled him through Cambridge with distinction, earning him recognition amongst peers twice his age.

Yet success felt hollow when weighted against the persistent ache in his chest.

Daniel's dark hair, neatly styled and befitting his professional status, caught droplets of morning mist as he navigated the cobbled pathways. His leather portfolio contained briefs for his first independent cases—property disputes and minor criminal matters that would establish his reputation. Everything he'd worked toward was finally within reach.

Everything except the one thing that mattered most.

Holly Clarke. The name whispered through his thoughts like a prayer, conjuring memories that refused to fade despite the passing years. Seven long years since that Christmas Eve fire had shattered her world, four years since she'd vanished completely from Hart House. Daniel had pursued every lead, followed every whisper, but each inquiry led to the same devastating conclusion.

Lady Cordelia Hart's tearful account never varied. Poor Holly had succumbed to consumption the previous winter, her grief-weakened constitution finally surrendering to illness. The funeral had been private, Cordelia claimed, attended only by family due to the contagious nature of her condition. No grave marker existed—the girl had been buried in the pauper's section, her exact location lost to bureaucratic indifference.

Daniel's magistrate father had accepted the explanation reluctantly. Sir Richard's initial suspicions about Holly's treatment had been impossible to prove, and Cordelia's performance had been thoroughly convincing. A grieving aunt, devastated by the loss of her sister's only child, overwhelmed by the responsibility she'd shouldered.

But something had always felt wrong about the story.

Daniel turned into the market district, his polished boots clicking against wet stones. Here, the city pulsed with genuine life—merchants hawking their wares, children darting between stalls, the mingled aromas of fresh bread and roasted chestnuts warming the cool air. Flower sellers lined the square's edges, their colorful displays brightening the grey morning.

This was where Daniel felt most useful, defending those who couldn't afford expensive representation. His father's wealth afforded him the luxury of choosing cases based on justice rather than profit, following the example set by Reverend Thomas Clarke all those years ago.

The memory stirred familiar guilt. Daniel had been just twelve when Holly's father died saving Mrs Bates, too young to understand the full implications of heroism. But he remembered the man's gentle wisdom, his unwavering commitment to those in need. Thomas Clarke had shaped Daniel's under-standing of true nobility—not the accident of birth, but the deliberate choice to serve others.

If only Daniel had been older when Holly needed protection. If only he'd recognised the danger lurking behind Cordelia's polished facade.

A splash of vibrant colour caught his attention near the square's far corner. A modest flower stall occupied the space between a fishmonger and a bread vendor, its display of autumn roses creating an island of beauty amongst the commercial chaos. The young woman tending the flowers moved with prac-tised efficiency, her auburn hair catching brief glimpses of sunlight that penetrated the morning mist.

Something about her profile made Daniel pause mid-stride.

The flower seller bent over her work, carefully arranging a bouquet of deep red roses with the sort of reverent attention usually reserved for sacred rituals. Her movements held a grace that transcended her simple surroundings—each stem posi-tioned with deliberate care, creating harmony from individual blooms.

Daniel's heart began to race without reason. The woman's profile stirred recognition he couldn't quite place, a familiar curve of cheek and jaw that pulled at memories buried deep. When she tucked a strand of hair behind her ear, the gesture was so achingly familiar that Daniel's breath caught.

"Excuse me," he called out, his voice carrying more urgency than he'd intended.

The young woman straightened slowly, turning toward his voice with apparent wariness. When her face came fully into view, time seemed to fracture around Daniel like shattered glass.

Green eyes. Unmistakable, brilliant green eyes that had haunted his dreams for years. Eyes that belonged to a girl supposedly dead and buried in an unmarked pauper's grave.

Eyes that now stared back at him with dawning recognition and something approaching terror.

"Holly?" The name escaped as barely more than a whisper, disbelief and desperate hope warring in his chest.

The flower seller—Holly Clarke, alive and standing mere feet away—went perfectly still. Her face had grown thinner over the years, marked by hardships Daniel could only imagine. But those eyes remained unchanged, windows to a soul he'd thought lost forever.

"Sorry I ..." Her voice carried the same breathless quality as his own, years of separation collapsing into this single moment of recognition.

Memory flooded back in vivid detail—a ten-year-old girl sharing her milk with stray cats, climbing apple trees with fearless joy, accepting his handkerchief with grateful tears when she scraped her knee. The same girl who'd endured unspeakable loss, then vanished into Cordelia Hart's web of lies.

Only she hadn't vanished. She'd been here all along, surviving in Ashford's forgotten corners whilst he'd mourned her death.

INVITATION

*H*olly squinted at the tall figure before her, struggling to reconcile the distinguished gentleman with fragments of memory that flickered like candle-light. He'd transformed from boy to man, bearing features she dimly recognised yet couldn't quite place. The formal black robes, the confident bearing—everything about him spoke of a world far removed from her flower stall.

"I ..." she stammered, her voice catching as emotions surged unbidden through her chest.

She studied his face, searching for familiar landmarks amongst the changes wrought by years. His jaw had strengthened, his shoulders broadened, yet something in his expression remained achingly familiar. The memories pressed against her consciousness like water against a dam, threatening to overwhelm her fragile composure.

Then his voice reached her again, warm and gentle despite the shock evident in his features.

"I bought eggs from you once, do you remember? I knew your father."

The words struck her like a physical blow. Holly gasped, her hand flying to her throat as the recollections crashed over her—a kind boy with concerned eyes, offering his precious handkerchief when she'd scraped her knee. The same boy who'd purchased all her eggs with such generous payment, whose gentle words about her father had been the first kindness she'd known since entering Cordelia's world.

Tears formed in her eyes, blurring the edges of the present moment. "Daniel," she whispered, the name carrying years of buried hope and impossible longing.

He stepped closer, his expression filled with wonder and something approaching anguish. "I tried to help then. I sent my father to Hart House, but then ..." His voice faltered, pain creasing his features. "They told us you died. Consumption, they said. We mourned you, Holly. I mourned you."

The revelation hit her like ice water. Cordelia had declared her dead, spinning lies to cover her escape. For four years, Daniel had believed her gone whilst she'd struggled to survive mere streets away from his home.

"I'm not dead," she managed, her voice barely audible above the market's din.

"No," he breathed, his eyes drinking in her face as though memorising every detail. "You're here. You're alive."

Daniel's gaze swept over her modest flower stall, her patched dress, the signs of hardship etched in her too-thin frame. When he looked back at her, determination had replaced the initial shock.

"Holly, would you ... would you join me for breakfast? I'll compensate for any lost sales. We have much to discuss."

The invitation hung between them, loaded with possibility and the weight of years apart.

BEGINNINGS

*H*olly's hands trembled as she followed Daniel through the bustling market toward a small café tucked between a haberdashery and a bookseller's shop. The morning crowd parted around them, and she felt acutely aware of her patched dress, her worn shawl, the scent of wildflowers clinging to her fingers. The café's painted sign creaked gently in the breeze, and through the mullioned windows, she glimpsed well-dressed patrons seated at polished tables.

"I shouldn't," she whispered, stopping just short of the entrance. "Look at me, Daniel. I don't belong in there."

Daniel turned, his expression gentle but firm. "You belong wherever kindness exists, Holly. You are worthy of any establishment in this town."

The café owner, a portly man with flour-dusted hands, glanced up as they entered. His eyes swept over Holly's appearance with obvious disapproval, but Daniel stepped forward with quiet authority.

"Good morning. Might we have a table for two? The lady has had a difficult morning."

Something in Daniel's bearing—the quality of his clothes,

the confidence in his voice—shifted the man's demeanour. "Of course, sir. Right this way."

They settled at a corner table beneath a painting of pastoral countryside. The gentle clink of china cups and murmured conversations created a cocoon of civilised warmth around them. Holly perched on the edge of her chair, hyperaware of every sound, every glance from other patrons.

"Tell me everything," Daniel said softly, once the owner had brought tea and warm scones. "What happened after that night you fled?"

Holly's fingers wrapped around the delicate teacup, drawing comfort from its warmth. The words came haltingly at first, then in a rush as four years of buried pain found voice. She told him about the cramped servant's room, the meagre meals whilst Cordelia feasted, the endless scrubbing until her hands bled raw.

Holly pressed on, describing the loose stone on the steps, the fraying well rope, each "accident" that might have killed her. When she reached the poisoned dinner and the cat's convulsions, Daniel's face went ashen.

"She tried to murder you?" The words came out strangled, barely controlled. "How could she treat you like that? You were a child—a grieving child."

His fists clenched on the table, and Holly saw the boy she'd once known blazing through the man's composure. The fierce protectiveness in his expression both comforted and frightened her.

"I'm sorry," he continued, his voice thick with anguish. "I should have done more. When Father visited Hart House and found nothing definitive, I should have pressed harder. I should have—"

"We were children, Daniel." Holly reached across the table, her fingers briefly touching his. "You tried to help. That's more than anyone else did."

Daniel shook his head, unconvinced. "I'll help now. I swear to you, Holly, I'll make this right."

He leaned forward, his voice dropping to ensure privacy. "There's something you need to know. Something you've never fully understood." He paused, choosing his words carefully. "You are not penniless, Holly. My father and I looked into it after hearing of your supposed death. Roseworth Cottage and your trust fund still exist."

Holly's teacup rattled against its saucer as her hands shook. "What do you mean?"

"The fund has grown considerably over time due to accumulated interest. You will inherit it all when you turn twenty-one —less than four years away."

The words struck her like physical blows. Holly stared at Daniel, her mind reeling. "But ... Cordelia said ..."

"Cordelia has been forced to wait. Because the circumstances of your death were uncertain—no body, no official certificate— she cannot legally claim the inheritance until after your twenty-first birthday would have passed. To do otherwise would raise suspicions." Daniel's eyes burned with determination. "But if we can build a legal case, prove what she did to you, you can reclaim everything."

Holly felt the world tilt around her. The café's warm chatter faded to a distant hum as the revelation settled into her consciousness. After years of believing herself truly orphaned and penniless, the possibility of reclaiming her birthright seemed almost impossible to comprehend.

"Four years," she echoed softly, the words strange on her tongue. A glimmer of something she'd thought lost forever— hope—began to kindle in her chest.

Yet even as her heart raced with possibility, caution wrapped around her like a familiar cloak. Four years on the streets had taught her that hope could be more dangerous than despair. Trust had become a luxury she couldn't afford, and even

Daniel's earnest expression couldn't entirely silence the voice that whispered warnings about believing too much, too quickly.

"I want to help you," Daniel continued, his voice urgent with sincerity. "Whatever it takes, however long it requires. You shouldn't have to face this alone."

Holly studied his face, searching for any sign of deception or ulterior motive. She found only the same kindness that had offered her a handkerchief years ago, now matured into something deeper and more resolute.

"Thank you," she said finally, her voice barely above a whisper. "For breakfast. For ... all of this."

She rose carefully, smoothing her patched skirt. "I hope to see you again. This time, hopefully without years in the interim."

Daniel stood as well, his expression both pleased and concerned. "You will. I promise you that, Holly. This isn't goodbye—it's the beginning of something better."

As Holly stepped back into the market's chaos, the café's warmth lingering on her skin, she allowed herself one small moment of possibility. Perhaps, after all these years of mere survival, she might finally have the chance to truly live again.

BUILDING TRUST

Over the following days, Daniel kept his word. Holly would be arranging flowers in her usual corner when his familiar silhouette would appear at the market's edge. He never approached directly, never disrupted her work, but simply waited until she acknowledged him with a cautious nod.

The first time he brought bread wrapped in clean linen, Holly's instinct was to refuse. Four years of survival had taught her that gifts always came with prices. But Daniel simply placed the parcel beside her flower basket and retreated to a respectful distance, his actions speaking louder than any reassurance.

When Holly unwrapped the bread that evening, sharing it with Nell and Benjamin beneath their usual bridge, she found herself describing Daniel's patient presence. Benjamin nodded approvingly whilst Nell remained sceptical.

"Gentleman like that don't help our sort without wanting summat back," Nell warned, though her tone carried more concern than suspicion.

Holly understood Nell's wariness. Yet each day, Daniel's consistency chipped away at her defences. He brought small offerings—a warm shawl when autumn's chill crept through the streets, a leather pouch to protect her Bible from rain. Never anything too grand that might embarrass her, but thoughtful gestures that spoke of genuine care.

What surprised Holly most was how Daniel interacted with the other street children. When little Jimmy approached one afternoon, curious about the well-dressed stranger, Daniel crouched to the boy's level and listened earnestly as Jimmy described his collection of interesting stones. Holly watched from across the market square as Daniel examined each pebble with the same attention he might give a precious gem.

"That one there," Daniel said, pointing to a smooth grey stone, "reminds me of the cliffs near Cambridge. Have you ever seen the sea, Jimmy?"

The boy shook his head, eyes wide with fascination as Daniel described rolling waves and endless horizons. Other children drifted closer, drawn by the magical pictures his words painted. Holly felt something tight in her chest begin to loosen as she witnessed his genuine delight in their company.

Three weeks after their café meeting, Daniel arrived carrying a leather satchel that bulged with promise. Holly had finished her flower sales early and sat against the weathered brick wall of an abandoned shop, watching the market's evening exodus.

"I thought you might enjoy these," Daniel said, settling beside her with careful attention to propriety's demands. The satchel opened to reveal a collection of well-worn books, their covers softened by countless readings.

Holly's breath caught. She hadn't held a proper book since fleeing Hart House, though her Bible remained her constant companion. These volumes spoke of adventures and distant lands, their spines bearing titles that stirred forgotten longings.

"Would you like me to read aloud?" Daniel asked, noting her hesitation. "I used to read to my younger cousins during holidays."

Holly nodded, not trusting her voice. Daniel selected a volume of fairy tales, its pages yellowed with age but illustrations still vibrant. As his voice rose and fell with the rhythm of the story, Holly felt herself transported beyond the market's grime and noise.

The tale spoke of a princess locked in a tower, but Daniel's reading breathed life into every word. His voice deepened for the dragon's roar, softened for the princess's lament, and sparkled with mischief during the clever prince's schemes. Holly found herself leaning closer, drawn into the narrative web he wove.

As the princess's garden bloomed beneath the tower window, Holly's mind drifted to her mother's gentle voice reading scripture by lamplight. The memory brought tears she quickly blinked away, but also a warmth she'd thought lost forever.

"Your mother read to you," Daniel observed softly, closing the book as the story concluded.

Holly nodded, surprised by his perceptiveness. "Every evening. She said stories were gifts that cost nothing to give but enriched everyone who received them."

"She sounds like she was a remarkable woman."

"She was." Holly's voice carried the weight of seven years' grief. "The stories made everything feel possible, even when life seemed impossible."

Daniel carefully placed the book back in his satchel. "Perhaps they still can."

As shadows lengthened across the market square, Holly realised something had shifted between them. The careful distance she'd maintained was dissolving, replaced by something warmer and more dangerous—trust.

SOMETHING TO LOSE

*T*he lodging house stood three storeys tall on Copper Lane, its brick facade weathered but solid. Holly's fingers trembled as she followed Daniel up the narrow staircase, past doors that muffled the sounds of other tenants—a baby's cry, an old man's cough, the scrape of chairs across wooden floors.

"The landlady mentioned this one receives good light," Daniel said, producing a brass key. "She's agreed to reasonable terms."

Holly's heart hammered against her ribs. For four years, shelter had meant doorways and abandoned buildings, spaces claimed temporarily before moving on. The idea of a room— her own room—felt too precious to believe.

Daniel opened the door and stepped aside, allowing Holly to enter first. The space was modest, barely large enough for the narrow bed pushed against one wall and the rickety table positioned beneath the window. But golden afternoon sunlight streamed through the glass panes, casting everything in warm amber that reminded Holly of her mother's kitchen at Roseworth.

"It's perfect," she whispered, though her voice caught on the words.

Over the following days, Holly transformed the bare room into something resembling home. She hung dried forget-me-nots from the market along the windowsill, their papery petals catching the light. A threadbare quilt that Mrs Patterson had pressed into her hands—payment for flowers when coins ran short—spread across the bed, its faded patchwork telling stories of other women's lives.

Daniel appeared each morning, helping her gather necessities from the market stalls. A small iron pot for cooking, chipped but serviceable. Two tin plates and cups that had seen better days but would suffice. Fresh bedding that smelled of lavender instead of the damp mustiness of the streets.

"You needn't spend so much," Holly protested as Daniel paid the stallholder for a woollen blanket.

"Consider it an investment," he replied with that gentle smile that made her pulse quicken. "Everyone deserves warmth."

The first evening in her new room, Holly heard familiar voices in the corridor outside. She opened her door to find Gracie and Tom—two children from their street family— huddled against the cold November rain, their thin clothes soaked through.

"Come in," Holly said without hesitation, stepping aside. "Both of you, quickly now."

They stumbled into the warmth, wide-eyed at the luxury of four walls and a roof that didn't leak. Holly wrapped them in her new blanket whilst she prepared a simple meal from her modest stores—bread still warm from the baker's oven, cheese that Daniel had insisted she purchase, and apples sweet with autumn's last promise.

Around the small table, they shared more than food. Tom regaled them with tales of a merchant's dog that had chased him through three streets after he'd tried to pet it. Gracie contributed observations about the market ladies' fashions, mimicking their affected speech until all three dissolved into laughter that filled the room with golden warmth.

As the children settled for sleep—Tom on the floor beside the bed, Gracie curled next to Holly beneath the quilt—Holly felt something shift inside her chest. This wasn't merely survival anymore. This was the beginning of something larger, a purpose beyond simply enduring each day.

Daniel's visits became as regular as sunrise. Each afternoon, after Holly finished selling her flowers, he would appear with books tucked under his arm or small treats from the bakery. They would sit by the window, sharing stories as daylight faded into dusk.

"Tell me about Cambridge," Holly would ask, watching his face animate as he described the ancient colleges and spirited debates with fellow students.

"Tell me about your ministry," he would counter, and Holly found herself speaking of the children who sought her out, the informal prayer services beneath the bridge, the way hope could flourish even in the darkest corners of the city.

With each conversation, the careful walls Holly had built around her heart crumbled a little more. Daniel's genuine interest in her thoughts, his respect for her work among the street children, his ability to see beyond her patched dress to the woman beneath—all of it conspired to kindle something dangerous within her.

Yet even as warmth bloomed between them, fear gnawed at Holly's contentment. In quiet moments, when Daniel's laughter still echoed in her room but he had gone home to Thornhill Manor, doubt crept in like winter fog.

She was a flower seller living in a rented room, sharing her bed with orphaned children. He was a barrister from a respected family, destined for prominence in county society.

The gulf between them stretched wider than the distance between the earth and stars.

What could someone like Daniel truly want with someone like her? Holly had watched gentlemen in the market, how they spoke to serving girls when they thought no one was looking. She had seen the aftermath when such attentions turned to abandonment, leaving young women ruined and destitute.

Late at night Holly stared at the ceiling and wrestled with possibilities too dangerous to voice. Perhaps Daniel's kindness masked expectations she couldn't fulfil. Perhaps his interest would wane once the novelty of her unusual circumstances wore thin.

The thought of losing this fragile happiness—her room, her purpose, the warmth in Daniel's eyes when he looked at her—made her stomach clench with familiar dread. She had survived abandonment before, but this felt different. This felt like something worth protecting, which meant it was something that could be lost.

CONNECTIONS

ord spread through Ashford's forgotten corners like wildfire. Within a month, Holly's modest room became a beacon for children who had nowhere else to turn. They arrived in twos and threes—shivering waifs clutching bundles of rags, their eyes holding that particular hollowness that came from too many nights sleeping rough.

"There's not enough space," Nell observed one evening, surveying the packed room where seven children had squeezed together on the floor.

"Then we'll make space," Holly replied, rearranging bedding yet again. She had given up her narrow bed entirely, sleeping on the floor beside the youngest ones who whimpered in their sleep.

Benjamin appeared in the doorway, his clubfoot making his approach audible on the creaking stairs. "Brought more bread," he announced, setting down a cloth bundle. "And Mrs Patterson sent soup bones for broth."

Together, the trio worked to transform the cramped quarters into something resembling sanctuary. Nell proved surprisingly adept at organising sleeping arrangements, whilst

Benjamin's gentle humour coaxed smiles from even the most frightened newcomers. Holly bustled between tasks—stirring soup, mending torn clothes, reading stories by candlelight.

"Tell us about the roses again," whispered Lucy, a girl of perhaps nine whose parents had died of fever.

Holly settled cross-legged on the floor, her worn Bible open in her lap. The candlelight flickered across young faces gathered in a circle, transforming the humble room into something sacred.

"My mother used to say that roses are the bravest flowers," Holly began, her voice carrying the cadence of countless retellings. "They push through thorns to reach the light. They bloom even when winter threatens, storing beauty in their hearts until spring returns."

"Like us?" asked Tommy, a boy whose stutter disappeared during these evening gatherings.

"Exactly like us," Holly confirmed, watching hope kindle in their eyes. "We may face thorns, but we're storing up beauty for when our spring comes."

The room filled with the soft murmur of children discussing their own springs—homes they dreamed of, families they hoped to find, trades they wished to learn. Holly felt her heart expand to encompass each fragile dream, each whispered prayer.

One grey afternoon, as December's chill crept through the window cracks, Daniel found Holly sitting alone by the glass. The children had scattered to their various pursuits—some begging, others running errands for shopkeepers willing to spare a penny.

"You look troubled," he observed, settling beside her on the floor.

Holly traced patterns on the dusty windowpane, her voice barely above a whisper. "I was thinking about the night I left Hart House. Running through those dark streets, not knowing if I'd see another dawn."

Tears gathered in her eyes like morning dew. "For so long, I felt invisible. As though I could disappear entirely and no one would notice. Cordelia certainly hoped I would."

Daniel's jaw tightened at the mention of her aunt, but his voice remained gentle. "You're not invisible, Holly. Not to these children, not to me."

"But what if—" Holly's voice cracked. "What if this is temporary? What if everyone leaves again?"

Daniel reached for her hand, his fingers warm against her cold ones. "Then we'll face whatever comes together. You're not that frightened girl running through the streets anymore. You've built something extraordinary here."

Holly met his gaze, finding steady conviction in his dark eyes. "Promise me something?"

"Anything."

"If you must leave—for your career, your family, any reason —tell me. Don't simply vanish like smoke."

"Holly." Daniel's voice carried the weight of an oath. "I'm not leaving. Not now, not ever. Whatever future awaits us, we'll navigate it side by side."

In the days that followed, Holly began to imagine possibilities she'd never dared consider. Safety—real safety, not merely the absence of immediate danger. A life where she could plan beyond tomorrow's bread, where dreams stretched further than simple survival.

Daniel seemed to sense this shift, guiding their afternoon walks through Ashford's better districts. They paused before shop windows displaying bolts of colourful fabric, watched children playing in proper gardens, observed families strolling together without fear.

"Look there," Daniel pointed to a small school where children emerged chattering excitedly. "Imagine what you could accomplish with proper resources. A real classroom, books, supplies."

Holly's breath caught. "You think I could teach?"

"I think you could move mountains if you set your mind to it."

The weight of his belief settled around her shoulders like a warm cloak. For the first time since her parents' death, Holly allowed herself to envision a future painted in colours brighter than grey survival.

Their conversations deepened as winter progressed. Daniel shared stories of Cambridge debates and legal principles, whilst Holly described the intricate dynamics of street life and the quiet miracles she witnessed daily among the children.

"You see people clearly," Daniel observed one evening as they watched Nell teach Lucy to plait her hair. "Their hearts, their potential. It's a rare gift."

Holly felt warmth bloom in her chest. "Mother used to say that everyone carries light inside them. Sometimes it just needs encouragement to shine."

"Like you've done for me," Daniel said quietly.

Holly turned to him in surprise. "What do you mean?"

"Before I met you again, I saw law as merely intellectual exercise. Now I understand its power to protect the vulnerable, to create justice for those who have none."

The realisation that their connection flowed both ways—that she had influenced him as profoundly as he had influenced her—filled Holly with wonder. Perhaps this wasn't charity or passing fancy. Perhaps what grew between them was something deeper, rarer, worth nurturing despite the obstacles ahead.

INVESTIGATION

*D*aniel spread the estate documents across his father's
oak desk, the lamplight casting harsh shadows over
columns of figures and legal signatures. His pen scratched
methodical notes as he traced each transaction, each supposedly
legitimate withdrawal from Holly's trust. The work consumed
him—breakfast forgotten, dinner cold on the tray his house-
keeper had brought hours earlier.

"Another guardian's fee," he muttered, examining a voucher
dated three months after Holly's supposed death. "Fifty pounds
for managing the estate of a deceased ward."

His jaw clenched as the pattern emerged with sickening clarity. Cordelia had been claiming expenses for Holly's care whilst
simultaneously reporting her dead. Educational fees for a girl
supposedly buried in the pauper's section. Medical bills for
treatments administered to a corpse.

The forgeries became obvious once Daniel knew what to
seek. Holly's signature—supposedly consenting to various
expenditures—bore no resemblance to the careful script he'd
seen in her Bible margins. The hand was too confident, too
practised. Cordelia's hand.

Daniel pulled the Roseworth trust documents toward him, comparing signatures line by line. The authentic ones from Holly's mother showed elegant, flowing letters. The recent additions were cruder imitations, clearly copied by someone unfamiliar with Mary Clarke's natural rhythm.

The sums involved made his stomach turn. Cordelia had systematically drained the trust over four years— never extremely large amounts, as to not be noticed, but enough to keep Hart House running whilst Geoffrey's gambling debts mounted. She'd used Holly's inheritance to maintain the very lifestyle that made her appear respectable to county society.

Daniel reached for a fresh sheet of paper, beginning to construct a timeline. Each fraudulent transaction, each forged signature, each false claim built a case so damning that no magistrate could ignore it. But something nagged at him—a lawyer's instinct that whispered of deeper crimes than mere theft.

He thought of Holly's stories about the "accidents." The loose stone, the frayed rope, the poisoned dinner. If Cordelia could forge documents with such calculated precision, what else might she have planned?

Daniel's pen paused over the ledger. A chill ran through him as he considered how close Holly had come to death. How convenient her demise would have been for Cordelia's schemes.

"Not just fraud," he whispered to the empty room. "Attempted murder."

The evidence lay before him like pieces of a puzzle, each document revealing another layer of Cordelia's deception. But Daniel knew gathering proof was only the beginning. The real challenge would be exposing a woman who had spent years perfecting the art of appearing blameless whilst orchestrating cruelty in shadows.

COMMUNITY

*H*olly knelt beside young Gracie, guiding the girl's small fingers as they arranged forget-me-nots into a proper bouquet. The morning light streamed through the lodging house window, illuminating the circle of children gathered around her makeshift table.

"See how the stems want to curve naturally?" Holly murmured, adjusting Gracie's grip. "Don't force them straight. Let them find their own way, then bind them gently."

Eight-year-old James watched intently from his perch on the windowsill, his own flowers scattered across his lap. "Like this, Miss Holly?"

"Perfect." Holly smiled as James held up his creation—a simple posy that would have made Benjamin proud. "Remember, each flower has its own story to tell. Your job is to help them tell it together."

The room buzzed with quiet concentration as seven children worked on their arrangements. Holly moved between them, offering encouragement and gentle corrections. What had begun as desperate survival had transformed into something richer—a community built on shared purpose and mutual care.

"Gracie, would you help little Sam with his stems?" Holly suggested, watching the older girl's face brighten with responsibility. "And Tom, perhaps you could show Mary how you've learned to tie the binding so neatly."

She'd discovered that the older children thrived when given charge over the younger ones. Thirteen-year-old Peter had appointed himself protector of the group, whilst eleven-year-old Annie naturally gravitated toward teaching the smallest children their letters. They weren't all here today, but that was always the way it was. Children — students — came and went, and Holly supplied for them when they needed her. Holly nurtured these instincts, understanding that leadership grew from service rather than authority.

A familiar knock interrupted her thoughts. Daniel appeared in the doorway, his arms laden with packages and his face brightening at the scene before him.

"Good morning, everyone," he called, setting down his burdens. The children chorused their greetings, no longer shy around the gentleman who brought books and treats.

"Mr Daniel!" Jimmy bounded forward, clutching a perfectly formed nosegay. "Look what I made! Miss Holly says I'm ready to sell them myself."

"Magnificent work." Daniel examined the flowers with the seriousness Jimmy deserved. "You'll earn good coin for these, I'm certain."

Holly watched Daniel's easy interaction with the children, her heart warming at his genuine interest in their small triumphs. He'd become more than a benefactor—he was family, woven into the fabric of their daily lives with the same care she tended her flowers.

"I've brought something special today," Daniel announced, producing a slate and chalks from his satchel. "Holly, I thought we might begin those reading lessons we discussed."

The children gathered eagerly as Holly cleared the table.

She'd dreamed of this moment—not just teaching letters, but opening doors to worlds beyond their cramped quarters. Daniel had helped her plan simple lessons that blended reading with practical skills, understanding that education meant survival for children like these.

"Today we'll learn words that help us sell flowers," Holly began, drawing careful letters across the slate. "Rose. Violet. Penny. Shilling."

As the children traced letters with their fingers, Holly caught Daniel's eye. His encouraging nod reminded her of possibilities she'd almost forgotten—dreams of a proper school, of children learning not from desperation but from hope.

Evening approached with its familiar rituals. Holly gathered the children in their customary circle, their small hands joining as they prepared for their nightly prayer. These moments had become sacred—not just words spoken to heaven, but bonds forged between souls who'd found family in unexpected places.

"Tonight we give thanks for new letters learned," Holly began, her voice steady and warm. "For flowers sold and bread earned. For friends who share our table and Mr Daniel's kindness."

"And for Miss Holly's stories," added Annie softly.

"And for not being caught by workhouse men," Peter contributed with the practical wisdom of his thirteen years.

Holly squeezed the hands holding hers. "And for tomorrow's possibilities, whatever they may bring."

The "Amen" that followed carried the weight of genuine gratitude. These children, who had every reason to despair, chose hope instead. Holly marvelled at their resilience—how quickly they'd learned to see abundance in their modest room, family in their circle of misfits.

Later, as the children settled into sleep, Daniel lingered by the window. Holly joined him, both gazing out at Ashford's lamplit streets.

"Word came to me today," Daniel said quietly. "Workhouse officials have been asking questions again. Someone reported a gathering of children in this district."

Holly's stomach tightened, but her voice remained calm. "What do you suggest?"

"I've spoken with Mrs Farthings downstairs. She's agreed to let the children slip into her cellar if officials come searching. The entrance is hidden behind her pantry—they'd never think to look there."

Holly nodded, grateful for his foresight. "Peter's already established signals. If anyone spots uniforms, we'll have warning."

They stood in comfortable silence, watching the city settle into darkness. Holly reflected on how much had changed since that terrifying night when she'd fled Hart House. Fear had given way to purpose, isolation to community.

"Holly." Daniel's voice carried a tenderness that made her heart flutter. "What you've built here—it's remarkable. These children look to you not because they must, but because they trust you completely."

She turned to face him, seeing something deeper than admiration in his dark eyes. "I couldn't have managed any of this without your help."

"You give me too much credit. The love in this room, the family you've created—that comes from your heart alone."

Spring was beginning to stir in the air beyond their window, promising renewal and growth. Holly thought of roses preparing to bloom again after winter's harshness, of children learning to read, of dreams taking shape in the most unlikely soil.

Her small room had become more than shelter—it was sanctuary, school, and home all woven together by threads of care and faith. Whatever challenges lay ahead, they would face them as they always had: together.

UNRAVELING

*C*ordelia Hart paced the drawing room. The afternoon light streaming through the tall windows seemed to mock her, illuminating dust motes that danced like specters in the air. She pressed her palms against her temples, trying to silence the whispers that had been following her through Ashford's streets for weeks.

"A young woman with auburn hair," Mrs Whitmore had mentioned at yesterday's tea. "Selling flowers in the market square. The strangest thing—she reminded me of dear Mary Clarke. Such a shame about her daughter though. What was her name ... Holly?"

Cordelia's reflection caught in the gilded mirror above the mantelpiece, and for a heart-stopping moment, she glimpsed another face staring back—green eyes filled with accusation, auburn curls framing features she'd thought buried forever. She spun away from the mirror, her breath coming in short gasps.

"Impossible," she muttered to the empty room. "Quite impossible."

But the rumours persisted, creeping through the town like ivy through stone. The flower girl who prayed. The young woman with gentle hands and a voice like music. Each detail carved another notch of terror into Cordelia's composure.

Across the room, Geoffrey slumped in his leather chair, the crystal tumbler in his trembling hands catching the light. His once-proud bearing had collapsed into something pitiful—shoulders curved inward, eyes sunken and bloodshot from sleepless nights and too much brandy. The man she'd married for his title and connections had withered into a hollow shell.

"The cat," Geoffrey mumbled, his voice thick with drink and despair. "Keep seeing the cat. Convulsions and foam and those terrible sounds."

Cordelia's jaw tightened. "Pull yourself together, Geoffrey. Your maudlin ramblings serve no purpose."

"No purpose?" He lifted his head, fixing her with watery eyes. "That poor creature died in agony. And the child—what we did to that child—"

"What we did?" Cordelia's voice turned glacial. "That ungrateful little wretch brought her circumstances upon herself. Wandering off in the night like some common vagrant."

Geoffrey's laughter held no mirth, only the bitter edge of a man who'd lost his way. "Vagrant. Yes, that's what she became, wasn't it? After we drove her to it."

The accusation hung between them like a sword. Cordelia felt her control fraying, threads of composure snapping one by one. She moved to the washstand in the corner, her movements sharp and purposeful.

The water was ice-cold against her palms, but she barely noticed. The bristled brush scraped against her skin as she worked it back and forth, back and forth, trying to cleanse something that couldn't be washed away. The phantom stains seemed to spread with each stroke—dark patches beneath her nails that no amount of scrubbing could remove.

"Blood," she whispered, her voice barely audible. "Still there. Always there."

The brush grew rough against her reddening skin, but she couldn't stop. The repetitive motion consumed her thoughts, drowning out Geoffrey's muttering and the whispers from town.

But even as she scrubbed, shadows moved in her peripheral vision. A flutter of auburn hair disappearing around a doorframe. The ghost of green eyes watching from darkened corners. Holly's presence seemed to seep through the walls of Hart House like morning mist, inescapable and accusing.

"You're not real," Cordelia hissed at the shadows.

The shadows didn't answer, but they didn't retreat either. They lingered at the edges of her vision, patient as death itself.

Dinner brought no respite. The dining room that had once showcased Cordelia's social triumphs now felt like a tomb, the ancestral portraits staring down with judgment in their painted eyes. Geoffrey picked at his food with the mechanical movements of a man who'd forgotten the taste of everything but guilt.

"Mrs Henshaw mentioned something curious today," Geoffrey ventured, his voice barely above a whisper.

Cordelia's fork paused halfway to her mouth. "Oh?"

"A young woman teaching children their letters. Gathering them for prayers under the old bridge." His watery gaze met hers across the table. "Auburn hair, she said. Green eyes like spring grass."

The fork clattered against Cordelia's plate. "Coincidence. Nothing more."

"Is it?" Geoffrey's question carried the weight of four years' accumulated doubt. "Because if she's alive—if she's been alive all this time whilst we've been claiming guardian fees—"

"She's dead." The words erupted from Cordelia with volcanic force. "Dead and buried and forgotten, just as she deserves."

But even as she spoke them, the words felt hollow. At night, when sleep eluded her completely, Cordelia lay rigid in her bed and imagined scenarios that made her blood run cold. Holly returning to claim Roseworth. Holly standing before magistrates, recounting every cruelty. Holly's testimony exposing the web of lies that had sustained them for four years.

The inheritance would be forfeit. The house would be lost. Cordelia's carefully constructed world would crumble into dust, and she would be left with nothing but the ashes of her ambition.

Her breath quickened in the darkness, each inhalation sharp and desperate. Somewhere in Ashford's labyrinthine streets, a ghost walked among the living. A ghost with auburn hair and accusing eyes, growing stronger with each passing day whilst Cordelia's sanity cracked like ice in spring.

The whispers would continue. The shadows would multiply. And somewhere in the distance, Cordelia could almost hear the sound of roses blooming from ashes.

DREAMS IN TWILIGHT

*T*he children scattered across the street like dandelion seeds on the wind, their laughter echoing off the lodging house walls as they clutched the makeshift slate pieces Holly had given them to practise their letters. Gracie turned back once, waving the precious chalk stub Daniel had brought, before disappearing around the corner with the others.

The evening light slanted through the narrow alley, casting everything in burnished gold—the cobblestones beneath her patched skirt, the weathered brick walls, even her own hands. After four years of surviving in shadows, she still marvelled at how beautiful the world could appear when touched by dying sunlight.

"Holly."

Daniel's voice carried a weight she'd never heard before, something deeper than their usual easy conversation. She looked up to find him standing a few paces away, his barrister's coat discarded and shirtsleeves rolled to his elbows. The golden light caught in his dark hair and softened the serious lines of his face.

"You are the most remarkable woman I have ever known."

The words fell between them like stones dropped into still water, sending ripples through the warm evening air. Holly felt her breath catch, not at the compliment itself but at the desperate sincerity threading through his voice, the way his hands trembled slightly at his sides.

A laugh escaped her, soft and breathless, tinged with an ache that settled deep in her chest. She gestured toward her patched dress, the worn shawl draped across her shoulders, the ink stains on her fingers from teaching children their letters with whatever scraps of paper and ink they could find.

"Remarkable?" The word felt foreign on her tongue. "I'm a flower seller, Daniel. You should be courting ladies in silk gowns, not wasting time with me."

Self-doubt crept through her words like morning mist, carrying with it the weight of every social barrier that stretched between them. She thought of the elegant ladies she glimpsed in the better districts of Ashford, their pristine gloves and unmarked hands, their confident laughter that had never known hunger or fear.

Daniel stepped closer, his expression fierce with conviction. "You're wrong."

His hand found hers, warm and steady, his fingers intertwining with her work-roughened ones without hesitation.

"Those ladies in silk gowns have never known hardship, never tested their faith, never sacrificed anything. You've faced the worst this world has to offer and remained kind, faithful, and generous. You are more of a lady than any of them will ever be."

Holly's pulse quickened beneath his touch, her carefully constructed defences crumbling like walls built of sand. She'd spent years burying her vulnerability beneath layers of determination and pride, but Daniel's words found every hidden crack, every secret hope she'd thought long dead.

"Daniel, I care for you deeply." The admission tore from her throat, raw and unguarded. "But we come from different worlds. Your family would never accept—"

"My father already knows everything."

The interruption came gentle but firm, his eyes burning with a determination that took her breath away. His hand tightened on hers, anchoring her as the world seemed to tilt beneath her feet.

"I told him about you, about what Cordelia did. He remembers your father saving Mrs Bates from that fire. He said any daughter of Thomas Clarke is welcome at Thornhill Manor, and he's prepared to testify on your behalf."

Holly stared at him, struggling to comprehend words that seemed too wonderful to be real. After years of believing herself forgotten, abandoned, worthless—to discover that someone remembered her father's sacrifice, that someone was willing to stand up for her ...

"I didn't want to move too fast though," Daniel continued, his voice gentling. "I didn't want to overwhelm or scare you away. I know you need time to learn to trust, but I'm willing to work for it as long as it takes."

Tears spilled down Holly's cheeks as a whirlwind of emotions crashed through her—hope and fear and joy all tangled together until she couldn't tell where one ended and another began. The possibility of justice, of reclaiming not just Roseworth but her very identity, ignited something within her that had lain dormant for so long she'd forgotten its name.

"A school," she whispered, the dream taking shape between them like something conjured from starlight. "I've always imagined running a proper school for children like these. Teaching them not just their letters but giving them hope, showing them they're worth something."

Daniel's eyes lit with understanding. "We could do it together. Your heart for teaching, my knowledge of law—we could create something that truly changes lives."

The words painted themselves across Holly's imagination in vivid strokes. Children with full bellies learning in warm rooms. Mothers knowing their little ones were safe and cared for. A place where birth didn't determine worth, where love mattered more than lineage.

"The old rectory beside Roseworth," she breathed, the vision growing clearer. "It has been empty since Father died. We could restore it, make it into classrooms. And the garden—Mother's roses could bloom again, and the children could learn about growing things."

"Your mother would be proud," Daniel said softly. "To see her daughter bringing beauty from ashes, just as she taught you."

Daniel stepped closer, his eyes tender as they searched her face. His free hand rose to cradle her cheek, thumb brushing away the tears that sparkled on her lashes like captured starlight.

"Holly."

Her name on his lips sounded like a prayer, like a promise. The warmth of his palm against her skin sent tremors through her that had nothing to do with the evening chill. She could smell the faint scent of his soap, see the way the golden light caught the flecks of amber in his brown eyes.

Without thinking, Holly tilted her face toward his, drawn by something deeper than conscious thought. Her pulse thundered in her ears as the distance between them shrank to nothing, as his breath whispered warm against her lips—

Terror crashed through her like ice water.

Holly jerked backwards, her hand flying to cover her mouth as though she could trap the moment before it escaped. Her chest heaved as panic flooded her veins, years of careful self-protection screaming warnings she couldn't ignore.

"I'm sorry." The words tumbled out broken and breathless. "Daniel, I'm so sorry, I can't—this is all so big, and after everything I've endured, after all the pain—"

Her voice cracked on the final word, and she wrapped her arms around herself as though she could hold her scattered pieces together. The walls she'd built to survive came crashing down around her, leaving her exposed and trembling in their ruins.

"Holly." Daniel's voice carried infinite gentleness as he stepped back, giving her the space her body was crying for. "You don't need to apologise."

His hands remained carefully at his sides, though she could see the effort it cost him in the tension of his shoulders, the way his fingers curled slightly as though fighting the urge to reach for her.

"I understand." Each word fell steady and sure, an anchor in the storm of her fear. "You've survived things that would have broken most people. Trust doesn't come easily after what you've endured, and I would never ask you to give what you're not ready to offer."

Holly lifted her eyes to his face, searching for any trace of frustration or disappointment. Instead, she found only patience, only the same steady kindness that had drawn her to him from the beginning.

"I'm willing to wait until the end of eternity for you," Daniel said softly. "However long it takes for you to feel safe, to feel free—that's how long I'll wait. Your comfort matters more to me than my own desires."

The words settled over Holly like a warm cloak, wrapping around the raw edges of her fear and soothing them into something bearable. She drew a shaky breath, feeling the tight coil of panic in her chest begin to loosen.

"Thank you." Her voice emerged barely above a whisper, but it carried the weight of everything she couldn't yet say—gratitude for his patience, wonder at his gentleness, amazement that someone could care enough to wait. "For understanding. For not pushing. For seeing me as more than my circumstances."

She wiped at her eyes with the back of her hand, suddenly aware of how she must look—tear-streaked and trembling, caught between hope and terror like a bird afraid to leave its cage even when the door stood open.

"I've spent so long protecting myself," she admitted, her gaze finding his and holding it despite the vulnerability that made her feel stripped bare. "Learning to trust again ... it frightens me more than Cordelia ever did."

Daniel nodded, his expression soft with understanding. "When you're ready, I'll be here. Whether that's tomorrow or years from now."

The golden light had faded to dusky purple around them, and Holly could hear Mrs Farthings calling for the children to come inside. The evening was ending, but something new had begun—fragile as a seedling, but rooted in soil rich with possibility.

SHADOWS AND SPECTRES

*T*he grandfather clock in Hart House chimed midnight, its resonant notes echoing through corridors that seemed to pulse with malevolent energy. Cordelia Hart sat rigid in her drawing room, still dressed in the burgundy silk she'd worn to Lady Pemberton's soirée hours earlier, though the elegant fabric now hung wrinkled and askew. Her fingers drummed against the mahogany armrest of her chair, each tap marking another frantic thought spiralling through her mind.

The flower girl. That cursed flower girl with Mary's auburn hair and those damning green eyes.

"I need watchers," she whispered to the empty room, her voice hoarse from the evening's forced pleasantries. "Someone reliable. Someone who understands the importance of ... discretion."

Her mind raced through possibilities—dockworkers, perhaps, or men who frequented the gambling dens where Geoffrey had accumulated his shameful debts. Surely amongst such company, she could find souls black enough to handle what needed handling. A few coins, a whispered suggestion that the flower girl posed a threat to proper society—surely that would suffice.

But even as she plotted, doubt gnawed at her resolve like acid eating through steel. What if they failed? What if this phantom girl truly was Holly, armed with memories and testimony that could destroy everything?

Cordelia's breathing quickened, her chest constricting as though invisible hands pressed against her ribs. Each plan felt more desperate than the last—hiring thugs to frighten the girl away, bribing officials to declare her mad, arranging an accident with a runaway cart. The schemes twisted through her thoughts like serpents, coiling tighter with each iteration.

"She's dead," Cordelia hissed, lurching to her feet with such violence that her chair toppled backwards. "I watched the consumption take her. I signed the death certificate myself."

But the lies tasted bitter on her tongue, and the shadows in the corners of the room seemed to shift and whisper accusations she couldn't quite hear.

A sound echoed from the hallway—footsteps, light and quick, like a child running through familiar corridors. Cordelia's head snapped toward the doorway, her pulse hammering against her throat.

"Who's there?" she called, her voice cracking on the final word.

Silence answered her, thick and oppressive.

Cordelia stumbled into the hallway. The lamps flickered, casting writhing shadows that seemed to mock her with their dance. In the gloom, she could swear she glimpsed a figure—small, slight, with hair that caught the weak light like burnished copper.

"Holly?" The name escaped her lips before she could stop it, raw and desperate.

The shadows shifted, and suddenly Cordelia could see them all—phantom children with hollow eyes and accusatory stares, their faces bearing the marks of hunger and neglect she'd inflicted through her cruelty. They pressed closer, their whispered voices joining in a chorus of condemnation that made her eardrums throb.

"No!" Cordelia shrieked, her hands flying to cover her ears. "You're not real! None of you are real!"

Her feet carried her stumbling toward the kitchen, where moonlight streamed through the windows and cast everything in silver and black. Her trembling fingers found the carving knife—the same blade she'd used to portion the small roast they had eaten just hours earlier. Now it felt heavy in her palm, its edge gleaming with promise.

"Get away from me!" she screamed at the shadows pursuing her, spinning wildly as she slashed at the empty air. The knife bit deep into the wallpaper, tearing through William Morris's delicate roses in savage strokes. "Leave me be! I did what I had to do!"

Her own reflection caught her eye in the kitchen's darkened window—wild-eyed and dishevelled, brandishing steel against phantoms only she could see. For a moment, she didn't recognise the creature staring back at her, this mad woman with her hair falling loose and her face twisted with desperate fury.

Cordelia's grip on the knife loosened, and it clattered to the floor with a sound like breaking bones.

MAKER CALLING

he wind cut through Daniel's coat as he approached
the modest cottage on Ashford's outskirts, its
thatched roof sagging under the weight of recent rains. Smoke
curled from the chimney in weak spirals, and the garden bore
the skeletal remains of autumn's last roses. He had spent the
better part of the last week tracking down Mrs Dawes through
enquiries at the market and conversations with former servants
who remembered the Hart household.

His knock echoed hollowly against the weathered oak door.
Footsteps shuffled inside—slow, careful movements that spoke
of age and infirmity. When the door creaked open, She
appeared fragile as parchment, her eyes sunken deep in her
skull.

"Who might you be, young man?" Mrs Dawes peered at
him through the narrow gap, her voice wavering with
suspicion.

"Daniel Thornhill, ma'am. Sir Richard's son." He removed his
hat, offering a respectful bow. "I'm a barrister, and I'm looking
into matters concerning Miss Holly Clarke."

The old woman's grip tightened on the doorframe, her

knuckles whitening. A tremor passed through her weathered features.

"Holly Clarke?" she whispered, the name falling from her lips like a prayer. "Sweet child ... what's become of her?"

"That's precisely what I hope to discover. Might I come in? I believe you once worked at Hart House."

Mrs Dawes stepped aside without another word, ushering him into a parlour barely larger than a pantry. The furniture was worn but clean, and a small fire struggled against the draft that seeped through the window frames. She lowered herself into a chair with obvious pain, gesturing for Daniel to take the seat opposite.

"She's alive then?" Mrs Dawes asked, her hands trembling in her lap. "Lady Cordelia claimed ... she said the child had died of consumption."

"Very much alive, and safe now. But I need to understand what happened at Hart House. What you witnessed."

Mrs Dawes closed her eyes, her breathing shallow and laboured. When she spoke again, her voice carried the weight of years held silent.

"I should've done more for that child," she began, tears sliding down her sunken cheeks. "God forgive me, I should've done more."

Daniel leaned forward, his barrister's instincts sharpening as he sensed the confession that was coming.

"The dinner," she continued, her voice breaking like glass. "That last dinner before she ran. I saw Lady Cordelia in the kitchen, hovering over the bowls like a hawk over prey. She sent me away on some errand—fetch wine from the cellar, she said— but something in her manner made me linger near the door."

Her hands wrung together, the skin so thin Daniel could see every vein beneath.

"I watched her pour something from a small brown bottle into Holly's bowl. Just a few drops, but I knew what it was.

Laudanum. Far too much for a child that size." She gasped, pressing a hand to her chest.

"The cat," Daniel said quietly, pieces falling into place.

"Aye, the cat. Poor creature ate from the bowl meant for Holly and died in such agony ..." Her voice dissolved into sobs. "The image haunts me still. Those convulsions, the way it writhed across the dining table. That should've been Holly. That should've been that dear child, and I nearly let it happen through my cowardice."

Daniel felt his jaw clench, fury building in his chest like a forge fire. "You saved her life, Mrs Dawes. Had you not acted—"

"I waited too long!" The words tore from her throat. "I suspected for months that something wasn't right. The way Lady Cordelia watched Holly, like she was measuring her for a coffin. The accidents that seemed to follow the child wherever she went. I told myself it was coincidence, that I was imagining things. But deep down, I knew."

She pressed her face into her hands, her frail shoulders shaking.

"I was meant to protect the innocent in that house, and I failed. I let fear keep me silent when I should've spoken. I let that monster masquerade as a caring aunt whilst she tortured that child for sport."

"Mrs Dawes, I must ask—would you be willing to provide testimony? To help bring Lady Cordelia to justice for what she's done?"

The old woman looked up at him, her eyes burning with a fever that seemed to consume her from within.

"I would gladly face the gallows myself if it meant seeing that woman pay for her crimes. But ..." She gestured weakly at her trembling hands, her laboured breathing. "I haven't much time left, Mr Thornhill. The physician says my heart won't see another spring."

"I should have brought Holly with me," Daniel said, reaching for her hand. "She would want to see you, to thank you."

"No." Mrs Dawes squeezed his fingers with surprising strength. "Better she remembers me as I was, not this broken shadow. Besides, I couldn't bear to look her in the eye, knowing how I failed her when she needed protection most."

Her breathing grew more ragged, and she leaned back in her chair with obvious exhaustion.

"You're her guardian angel now, aren't you? I can see it in the way you speak of her. Promise me you'll do better than I did. Promise me you'll keep her safe from those who would harm her."

"I promise," Daniel whispered, his throat tight with emotion.

Mrs Dawes smiled then, the first genuine peace he'd seen cross her features. She struggled to sit straighter, her eyes bright with newfound purpose despite her failing body.

"Help me to the writing desk," she whispered, gripping the arms of her chair. "If I'm to make amends, it must be now."

Daniel assisted her trembling form across the small room to a battered wooden desk near the window. She lowered herself into the chair with a sharp intake of breath, her fingers fumbling for paper and pen amongst the scattered belongings.

"Tell me what to write," she said, her voice gaining strength from determination. "I may not live to see the courtroom, but my words will speak for that child."

Daniel positioned himself beside her, watching as she dipped the pen with shaking hands. Ink spotted the paper as she struggled to maintain control.

"Begin with your name and position at Hart House," he instructed gently.

Her script wavered like autumn leaves, but each word carried the weight of her confession. She detailed the laudanum, the cat's agonising death, the accidents that had plagued Holly's time under Cordelia's roof. Sweat beaded on her brow from the effort, but she pressed on relentlessly.

"There," she gasped, setting down the pen. "Let this be my testimony when I cannot speak for myself."

Daniel slipped his arm beneath Mrs Dawes's elbow, feeling how frail she'd become beneath her worn shawl. Her legs trembled with each step, and he bore most of her weight as they moved from the desk to her chair by the fire.

"Easy now," he murmured, lowering her gently into the cushioned seat. Her breathing came in shallow gasps, each exhale a visible puff in the cottage's chill.

She sagged against the chair back, her face pale as winter frost. The effort of writing had drained what little strength remained in her failing body.

"You can rest now," Daniel said, adjusting the blanket across her lap.

"Will you stay with me, Mr Thornhill? I feel my maker calling, and I don't want to meet Him alone. Perhaps He'll forgive this old woman's cowardice when He sees the good man standing watch."

Daniel settled back in his chair, taking her frail hand in his steady grip. As Mrs Dawes drew her final breath with the setting sun painting the cottage walls gold, a single tear traced down his cheek for the woman who had saved Holly's life and carried the guilt of it to her grave.

HAVEN OF HOPE

*T*he small room on Copper Lane had transformed beyond recognition. What began as Holly's solitary refuge now overflowed with eager faces each evening, children ranging from tiny waifs of six to hardened survivors approaching adulthood. Tonight, seventeen souls crowded into the space that barely accommodated five, yet somehow the walls seemed to expand with their shared warmth.

Holly knelt beside eight-year-old Maisie, guiding the girl's grimy finger across the page of her father's Bible. "Sound it out slowly," she encouraged, watching Maisie's brow furrow in concentration.

"F-a-i-t-h," Maisie pronounced carefully, then looked up with triumph shining in her dirt-streaked face. "Faith!"

A chorus of approval rose from the other children, and Holly felt her heart swell. Three months ago, Maisie couldn't recognise a single letter. Now she read simple passages with growing confidence.

"That's exactly right," Holly said, squeezing the child's hand. "And what does faith mean?"

"Believing in something good, even when you can't see it

yet," piped up Jimmy from his place by the window, where he'd been arranging stones in careful patterns whilst listening.

Holly nodded, watching as older children helped younger ones with their slate work. Peter, now nearly fifteen, had become her unofficial assistant, demonstrating letter formations with patient repetition. Annie, despite being only twelve herself, naturally gravitated toward the smallest children, reading them simple stories in a voice that could soothe the most fractured spirit.

They were building something together—not just lessons, but a family bound by shared struggle and mutual care.

"Tell us about the loaves and fishes again," requested Sarah, a newcomer who'd appeared three nights ago with haunted eyes and clothes hanging in tatters.

Holly opened to the familiar passage, but before she could begin, Benjamin's signal carried up from the street. Their agreed signal—three sharp whistles followed by two long ones. Workhouse officials.

The children moved with practised efficiency, gathering their few possessions and slipping down to Mrs Farthing's pantry. Mrs Farthings had prepared the cellar beneath her bakery for such moments, and Peter led the exodus with quiet authority.

Holly waited until the last child disappeared into the night before dousing the candles. In the sudden darkness, she pressed her forehead against the cool window glass and watched shadows move through the alley below. Grey uniforms, searching methodically.

They'd found others recently—children who'd vanished into the workhouse system, never to be seen again. The thought made her stomach clench with familiar dread.

A gentle knock interrupted her vigil. Daniel's voice, soft and careful: "Holly? It's safe now. They've moved on."

She opened the door to find him holding a small oil lamp,

concern etched across his features. Behind him, the children began trickling back, their relief palpable.

"How did you know to come?" she asked as the little ones settled back into their makeshift circle.

"Benjamin sent word. I was at the magistrate's office, working on ..." He paused, glancing at the children. "Legal matters. I came as quickly as I could."

Their eyes met across the crowded room, and Holly felt that familiar flutter in her chest—half warmth, half panic. For weeks now, Daniel had been patient beyond measure, never pressing for more than she could give. He brought books and treats, listened to her dreams of a proper school, shared his own hopes of using law to protect the vulnerable.

Yet when he stepped closer, when his fingers accidentally brushed hers whilst passing a slate, she still flinched away like a startled sparrow. The betrayal she'd endured at Hart House had carved deep trenches in her ability to trust completely, even with someone as gentle as Daniel.

"Read to us, Mr Daniel," called out Tom, settling against the wall with obvious weariness.

Daniel looked to Holly for permission, and she nodded, grateful for the distraction from her churning thoughts. As his voice filled the room with tales of brave knights and distant kingdoms, Holly watched the children's faces transform from wariness to wonder.

This was what mattered—these souls who depended on her, this small haven of hope they'd built together. Her heart might struggle with the complexity of love, but here amongst the candles and whispered prayers, she knew exactly who she was meant to be.

ACT OF MERCY

*T*he gaslight flickered against the drawing room walls, casting wavering shadows that seemed to mock Cordelia's every movement. She paced from the mahogany sideboard to the marble fireplace, her silk slippers whispering against the Persian carpet with each measured step. The house felt smaller tonight, as though the very walls were closing in around her carefully constructed existence.

Holly Clarke. The name hammered against her skull like a death knell.

Cordelia's reflection caught in the darkened window—pale, sharp-featured, but with something wild lurking behind her composed exterior. She pressed her fingertips against the glass, feeling the cold seep through to her bones.

The investigator had been easy enough to find. Men like Xavier Grimm gravitated toward the seedier taverns where questions weren't asked and coin spoke louder than conscience. The Boar's Head reeked of stale ale and unwashed bodies, but Cordelia had endured worse for her purposes.

"Find her," she'd whispered across the sticky wooden table, sliding a leather purse toward his grimy hands. "The flower girl in the market district. Auburn hair, green eyes, teaches the guttersnipes their letters."

Grimm's yellowed teeth had glinted in the tavern's smoky light. "And what would you be wanting with such a creature, m'lady?"

"That needn't concern you. Merely locate her dwelling, her habits, her ... vulnerabilities." The coins clinked as he weighed the purse. "There's twice that amount waiting when you bring me what I require."

Now, three days later, Cordelia's nerves stretched taut as piano wire. Each footstep in the corridor might herald Grimm's return with news that would either save or damn her.

The study door creaked open, and Geoffrey shuffled in, his waistcoat stained with brandy and his eyes bloodshot from another evening's indulgence. He'd grown worse since the cat died, muttering about phantoms and justice, his guilt eating him alive like a cancer.

Perfect.

"Geoffrey, darling," Cordelia purred, moving to pour him another drink. "I've been thinking about the rumours of that poor creature."

His hand trembled as he accepted the glass. "What creature?"

"The one who looks so remarkably like dear Holly. The resemblance is quite ... disturbing." She settled beside him on the leather sofa, her voice dropping to concerned whispers. "I fear seeing her has affected you terribly. The way you've been speaking lately, the things you imagine ..."

Geoffrey's pale eyes darted toward her. "I haven't imagined anything."

"Haven't you?" Cordelia's fingers traced patterns on his sleeve. "The nightmares, the guilt, the way you see things that aren't there. And now this girl appears, stirring up memories that should remain buried."

She watched his face crumble, the brandy and her words working their poison through his already fractured resolve.

"Perhaps," she continued, her tone gentle as a mother's lullaby, "it would be kindest to have her evaluated. Professionally. Young women living rough often develop ... disturbances of the mind. Delusions. They begin believing themselves to be people they're not."

Geoffrey's breathing quickened. "You think she's mad?"

"I think she's suffering, my dear. And if she truly resembles Holly so closely, imagine the torment it must cause her—and us. Society has ways of caring for such troubled souls. Quiet places where they can find peace."

The gaslight dimmed, and Cordelia felt a familiar thrill course through her veins. Like a spider spinning her web, each thread carefully placed to ensnare her prey.

"It would be an act of mercy," she whispered, "for everyone involved."

EMPIRE OF LOYALTY

*X*avier Grimm spat into the gutter and pulled his coat tighter against the chill. Three days of watching the flower girl had yielded more than he'd bargained for. The auburn-haired lass wasn't just some mad beggar spinning tales —she'd built herself a proper little kingdom amongst the dregs of Ashford.

He crouched behind a stack of empty crates, yellow teeth worrying at a splinter of wood whilst his rheumy eyes tracked the girl's movements. Holly Clarke—if that were truly her name —arranged forget-me-nots with the careful attention of a lady arranging roses in Mayfair. The irony wasn't lost on him.

"Maisie, mind the stems don't snap," the girl called to a waif of eight or nine. "Benjamin showed us how they tell stories when they're whole."

Stories. Grimm snorted. The street children clustered round her like moths to a flame, hanging on every word as though she were some sort of saint. He'd counted seventeen of the little vermin over the past days—all devoted to their "Miss Holly" with a fervour that bordered on worship.

The Welsh lad with the clubfoot appeared from behind a

fishmonger's stall, his arms laden with wilted blooms rescued from the day's refuse. Benjamin, they called him. The girl's lieutenant, near enough. Grimm had watched him orchestrate the children's movements with military precision—who went where, when to scatter, how to signal danger.

Then there was the other one. Nell. Sharp as a blade and twice as dangerous, with eyes that missed nothing. She'd spotted Grimm twice already, forcing him to skulk deeper into the shadows like a common thief.

But it was the gentleman visitor that truly confounded him.

Every afternoon, regular as clockwork, a young man in barrister's robes appeared at the girl's flower stall. Daniel Thornhill, if the whispers were accurate. Son of Sir Richard, the magistrate. Grimm had observed their conversations—earnest, intimate, charged with something that looked suspiciously like affection.

The girl wasn't mad. That much was crystal clear. She was organised, respected, connected to people of influence. Lady Hart's delicate flower girl had roots that ran deeper than expected, tendrils that stretched into places where yellow-toothed investigators feared to tread.

Grimm pulled the leather notebook from his coat and scrawled his observations with a stubby pencil. Countless children under her protection. Two devoted companions. A magistrate's son paying court. Evening gatherings in the lodging house on Copper Lane where she read from a battered Bible.

The flower girl who prays indeed.

Lady Hart had hired him to find vulnerabilities, but what he'd discovered was an empire of loyalty built on kindness and hope. Dismantling such a thing would require more than whispered accusations and forged papers.

It would require destroying everything she'd built.

CONSULTATION

*C*ordelia pressed her gloved fingers against the consulting room door, steadying herself before stepping into the gaslit corridor of Dr Creighton's practice. The physician's reassurances still rang in her ears—yes, the committal papers could be prepared discreetly; yes, disturbed young women often required institutional care; yes, family members frequently sought such arrangements out of compassion rather than malice.

The fog had thickened during her appointment, transforming Harley Street into a maze of shadows and muffled sounds. Cordelia pulled her cloak tighter, her mind already calculating the next steps. Grimm's report lay folded in her reticule—a multitude of witnesses to the girl's supposed delusions, a magistrate's son who might complicate matters, but nothing that couldn't be managed with the right documentation and Dr Creighton's professional opinion.

She stepped into the swirling mist, her boots clicking against the wet cobblestones. The familiar weight of the laudanum bottle nestled in her pocket provided cold comfort. If the asylum plan failed, there were other methods. More permanent solutions.

A gentleman emerged from the fog ahead, his tall frame silhouetted against the amber glow of a street lamp. Cordelia's breath caught in her throat as recognition struck like a physical blow.

Daniel Thornhill.

The magistrate's son moved with purpose down the sidewalk, a leather satchel tucked beneath his arm. His dark eyes swept the area with the methodical attention of someone conducting business rather than pleasure. When their gazes met, Cordelia felt her carefully constructed composure threaten to crumble.

"Lady Hart." Daniel's voice carried the crisp authority of his Cambridge education. He executed a polite bow, though his expression remained guarded. "I hadn't expected to encounter you in this district."

Cordelia forced her lips into what she hoped resembled a gracious smile. Her pulse hammered against her throat as she searched for an explanation that wouldn't invite scrutiny.

"Mr Thornhill. How ... unexpected." She adjusted her grip on her reticule, acutely conscious of the papers within. "I've been consulting with Dr Creighton regarding charitable endeavours. The poor souls in our workhouses often require medical attention beyond what their facilities can provide."

The lie tumbled from her lips with practised ease, though she detected a flicker of something—suspicion?—in Daniel's dark eyes. He stepped closer, and Cordelia caught the scent of leather and ink that clung to his clothes.

"How commendable." His tone remained perfectly polite, yet something beneath the surface made Cordelia's skin crawl. "Though I confess surprise at finding you here personally. Surely such arrangements could be handled through correspondence?"

Heat flooded Cordelia's cheeks despite the November chill. "One finds that personal attention yields better results in matters of ... delicate concern. These unfortunate creatures often require specialised care that demands careful explanation."

"Indeed." Daniel's gaze sharpened. "I've been conducting some research myself into the welfare of Ashford's more vulnerable residents. Street children, particularly. Amazing how many slip through the cracks of our charitable institutions."

The words struck Cordelia like ice water. She fought to keep her expression neutral whilst her mind raced through possible connections. Had Grimm been discovered? Did Daniel suspect the true nature of her inquiries?

"Street children?" She infused her voice with appropriate concern. "How dreadful. Though I suppose such creatures are naturally drawn to ... unsavoury influences. The poor dears often develop quite fanciful notions when left to their own devices."

"Fanciful notions?" Daniel's eyebrows rose slightly.

"Oh yes." Cordelia leaned forward conspiratorially, her voice dropping to a sympathetic whisper. "Delusions of grandeur, claims of noble birth, tales of persecution. The physician was just explaining how grief and hardship can so easily unbalance young minds. Particularly in girls who've suffered familial loss."

Daniel's jaw tightened almost imperceptibly. "How ... illuminating."

Cordelia pressed her advantage, weaving truth into deception with the skill of a master seamstress. "Dr Creighton mentioned several such cases—poor creatures who've convinced themselves they're someone they're not. Often they gather followers amongst other unfortunates, spreading their fantasies like some sort of ... contagion."

"And these girls would require institutional care?"

"For their own protection, naturally." Cordelia's voice

dripped with manufactured compassion. "Professional evaluation, proper treatment. One cannot allow such disturbances to fester amongst the vulnerable population. The consequences could be quite ... unfortunate."

Daniel studied her face with uncomfortable intensity. In the lamplight, his features appeared carved from stone, revealing nothing of his thoughts. Cordelia felt exposed, as though he could peer directly into her skull and read the calculations churning within.

"How fortunate that concerned citizens like yourself take such interest in these matters," he said finally.

"One must do one's Christian duty." Cordelia clutched her reticule tighter, desperate to escape his scrutiny. "Though I fear I've detained you overlong. Such fog makes travel treacherous."

"Indeed it does." Daniel's smile held no warmth. "Good evening, Lady Hart. I trust your ... charitable endeavours prove successful."

He tipped his hat and melted back into the swirling mist, leaving Cordelia alone with her hammering heart and churning thoughts. Had she said too much? Revealed her hand? The encounter felt like a chess match where she couldn't determine whether she'd gained ground or walked directly into checkmate.

Behind her, Dr Creighton's practice windows glowed amber in the fog. The papers waited within, requiring only her signature and the girl's capture committal. But Daniel Thornhill's knowing eyes haunted her thoughts as she hurried through the darkened streets toward Hart House.

The game had grown more dangerous than she'd anticipated.

SHADOWS

*H*olly knelt beside little Maisie on the worn floorboards of her lodging room, guiding the child's finger beneath each word as they read together from the Gospel of Matthew. The candlelight flickered across the pages, casting dancing shadows that seemed to move independently of the flame.

"Blessed are the meek," Maisie whispered, her voice trembling with concentration, "for they shall inherit the earth."

"Beautiful, love." Holly squeezed the girl's thin shoulder. "Your reading improves every day."

Around them, nine children clustered in the small space—some perched on the narrow bed, others cross-legged on the floor. Peter helped young Tommy with his letters whilst Annie braided Sarah's hair. The room hummed with quiet industry and contentment.

A sound outside the window caught Holly's attention. She glanced up from the Bible, her gaze searching the darkened street beyond the glass. Nothing. Only shadows pooling between the lampposts and the usual bustle of evening pedestrians hurrying home.

Yet the sensation persisted—a prickle between her shoulder blades, as though unseen eyes tracked her movements. For three days now, this feeling had haunted her. Each time she arranged flowers in the market square, each time she led the children to their hiding place in Mrs Farthings' basement, that crawling awareness followed.

"Miss Holly?" Maisie tugged at her sleeve. "Are we finishing the story?"

Holly forced her attention back to the child's expectant face. "Of course, darling."

But even as she continued reading, her peripheral vision remained alert. Yesterday, whilst sorting wildflowers at her stall, she'd caught a glimpse of a figure ducking behind the fishmonger's cart. The day before, someone had lingered too long near the bakery whilst she purchased bread for the children.

When Benjamin arrived an hour later with his basket of woven flowers, Holly pulled him aside.

"Have you noticed anything ... unusual?" she asked quietly, mindful of the children nearby. "Anyone watching us?"

Benjamin's weathered face creased with concern. "Nell mentioned something. Said she spotted a gentleman near the old bridge during prayers last night. Thought it strange—not the usual sort who comes to listen."

Holly's stomach clenched. "What did he look like?"

"Couldn't see clearly in the lamplight. But Nell's instincts are sharp. If she sensed something amiss ..."

The words hung between them, heavy with implication. Holly glanced at the children, their faces bright with innocence as they practised their letters. The thought of danger touching them made her chest tighten.

"There's something else," Benjamin continued, his voice dropping lower. "Tom heard whispers at the market today. About Lady Hart."

Holly's blood chilled. "What sort of whispers?"

"Folk saying she's been ... unwell. Acting strange. Mrs Patterson mentioned seeing her at odd hours, walking the streets alone. Talking to herself."

The image of her aunt's cold blue eyes flashed through Holly's memory—calculating, ruthless. If Cordelia suspected Holly's survival, if she'd discovered the refuge on Copper Lane ...

"We should tell Daniel," Benjamin said.

Holly nodded, though anxiety coiled in her stomach. These past weeks with Daniel had been precious beyond measure—his gentle patience, his encouragement of her teaching, the way his eyes lit when she spoke of her dreams for the children. Trust had begun to bloom in her heart like her mother's roses after winter.

But trust felt fragile when shadows followed her through the streets.

"Miss Holly!" Gracie called from across the room. "Will you tell us about the loaves and fishes again?"

Holly smiled, pushing her fears aside for the children's sake. "Gather around, little ones."

As the children settled in a circle, Holly began the familiar tale. But even as she spoke of miracles and abundance, her gaze drifted repeatedly to the window. The darkness beyond seemed deeper tonight, more threatening.

Somewhere in that darkness, she felt certain, someone watched and waited.

THE WEB TIGHTENS

*C*ordelia received Xavier Grimm in her private sitting room at precisely nine o'clock, the gas lamps turned low to discourage any servant from lingering near the door. The investigator stood before her fireplace, his wiry frame casting sharp angles against the flickering light. In his weathered hands, he held a leather portfolio that would determine Holly Clarke's fate.

"Your report, Mr Grimm." Cordelia's voice carried the crisp authority of a woman accustomed to purchasing loyalty.

Grimm opened the portfolio with deliberate precision. "The girl has established quite the operation, my lady. Far from the destitute beggar you described." He withdrew a sheet of closely written notes. "She maintains lodgings on Copper Lane, runs what amounts to a school for street children, and conducts regular prayer meetings beneath the old bridge."

Cordelia's fingers drummed against her chair's velvet arm. "How many children?"

"Seventeen at last count. They follow her with remarkable devotion. The older ones—a Welsh lad with a clubfoot and a sharp-eyed girl called Nell—serve as her lieutenants. They've created an effective warning system against workhouse officials."

"And her ... protector?"

"Daniel Thornhill visits daily. The son shows considerable attachment to the girl." Grimm's expression remained neutral, though his tone suggested disapproval. "He brings supplies, assists with lessons, reads to the children. Their relationship appears ... intimate."

Cordelia's jaw tightened. The Thornhill name commanded respect throughout the county. If Daniel involved himself in Holly's affairs, the complications would multiply exponentially.

Grimm reached into the portfolio again. "I obtained this from a street photographer who frequents the market district."

He handed Cordelia a small photographic plate. The image showed Holly surrounded by laughing children, a crown of wildflowers adorning her auburn hair. Her face glowed with genuine happiness, her green eyes bright with purpose. The children gazed at her with unmistakable adoration.

Cordelia's vision blurred with sudden rage. Here was Holly Clarke—her orphaned niece who should have died years ago— thriving amongst the very people Cordelia dismissed as vermin. The girl who possessed Roseworth Cottage and a fortune that grew daily with compound interest appeared radiant, beloved, successful.

"She looks ... content," Cordelia managed, her voice barely controlled.

"More than content. She's built an empire of loyalty through kindness. The children would die for her."

The photograph trembled in Cordelia's grip. Holly wore a patched dress that cost less than Cordelia's morning gloves, yet she appeared more regal than any duchess. The injustice of it— this slip of a girl commanding such devotion whilst Cordelia fought to maintain appearances in Hart House—ignited something vicious in her chest.

"Leave me." The words emerged as a whisper.

Grimm collected his payment and departed without ceremony. Alone in the sitting room, Cordelia began to pace before
the dying fire, her silk skirt rustling with each sharp turn. The
photograph lay abandoned on the side table, Holly's joyful face a
constant accusation.

Roseworth Cottage. The words echoed in Cordelia's mind like
a prayer turned curse. The estate that should have been hers,
inherited by Mary through their grandmother's spite. The trust
fund that accumulated interest year after year, growing beyond
Cordelia's wildest dreams whilst she struggled with Geoffrey's
gambling debts.

Holly remained ignorant of her wealth, believing herself a
penniless flower girl. But in less than four years, on her twenty-
first birthday, she could inherit everything. Roseworth. The
funds. The power to destroy Cordelia's carefully constructed
life.

Unless ...

Cordelia paused before her writing desk, excitement and
malice coursing through her veins like wine. The solution crystallised with perfect clarity—not crude violence or obvious
poison, but an elegant trap that would eliminate Holly whilst
maintaining Cordelia's reputation.

She withdrew expensive stationery and began composing the
first of several letters. Her pen moved with practised elegance as
she crafted a fictitious correspondence from Lady Pemberton to
Mrs Whitworth, detailing a mysterious benefactress who wished
to fund charitable works amongst Ashford's poor children.

*"The lady in question has recently inherited a substantial fortune
and seeks worthy causes for her philanthropy. Young women engaged
in educational ministry particularly capture her interest, as she herself
was orphaned at a tender age ..."*

The lies flowed like honey from her pen. She described

generous monthly stipends, proper schoolrooms, warm clothing for the children, and trained teachers to assist with lessons. Everything Holly Clarke would desperately want for her little flock.

By midnight, Cordelia had composed five letters to prominent women in Ashford's charitable circles, each slightly different but weaving the same tantalising story. The mysterious benefactress wished to meet with Miss Clarke privately to discuss funding arrangements. A reputable solicitor's office had been arranged for the consultation.

Of course, no such solicitor existed. The address would lead Holly directly into Cordelia's waiting hands.

The following evening, Cordelia met with Mrs Adelaide Foster and Miss Catherine Henley in the conservatory of Mrs Foster's townhouse. Both women owed Cordelia significant social debts—invitations to exclusive gatherings, introductions to influential connections, assistance with their daughters' marriage prospects.

"I require your discretion in a delicate matter," Cordelia began, her tone suggesting grave importance. "A dear friend has asked me to identify worthy recipients for her charitable endeavours."

Mrs Foster leaned forward eagerly. Charitable works enhanced one's reputation considerably.

"There is a young woman in Ashford," Cordelia continued, "who has dedicated herself to educating street children. My friend wishes to support such noble efforts, but anonymity remains essential. She prefers to evaluate potential recipients personally before committing substantial funds."

Miss Henley nodded sagely. "Wise precaution. So many fraudulent appeals these days."

"Indeed. I need reliable intermediaries to approach this Miss Clarke—Holly Clarke, I believe her name is. Someone must convey the benefactress's interest whilst maintaining complete confidentiality."

Cordelia withdrew a sealed envelope. "The meeting is arranged for tomorrow at six o'clock in the evening. The address is contained within, along with specific phrases to ensure Miss Clarke understands the sincerity of the offer."

She pressed the envelope into Mrs Foster's gloved hands. "Tell her that 'roses bloom brightest after harsh winters.' She will understand the reference and trust the source."

"And if she hesitates?" Miss Henley asked.

Cordelia's smile could have frozen champagne. "Emphasise the children's needs. Their hunger, their lack of proper shelter, their desperate circumstances. Miss Clarke possesses a tender heart—perhaps too tender for her own good."

"We must act quickly before the girl realises the danger she is in," Cordelia added, though neither woman grasped the true meaning behind her words.

Cordelia returned to Hart House with triumph singing in her veins. Tomorrow, Holly Clarke would walk willingly into the trap that would end her inconvenient existence forever.

BRIGHT POSSIBILITY

*H*olly knelt beside eight-year-old Jim, guiding his small fingers as he traced letters in the dust beside the flower stalls. The afternoon sun cast long shadows across the market square, and most vendors had begun packing their wares.

"J-I-M," Holly said softly. "Your name has the tallest letter in the alphabet."

Jim's face brightened. "Like a giant!"

"Exactly like a giant." Holly smoothed away the letters and began drawing a simple flower. "Now show me what this is."

"Rose!" Jim exclaimed, then his voice grew quieter. "Like the ones you tell stories about."

Before Holly could respond, two well-dressed ladies approached their makeshift classroom. Holly recognised Mrs Foster from charitable gatherings at the parish, though they had never spoken directly. The other woman, elegant in deep blue silk, remained unfamiliar.

"Miss Clarke?" Mrs Foster's voice carried the refined tones of Ashford's better districts. "Might we have a word?"

Holly rose, brushing dust from her patched skirt. Jimmy

scrambled to his feet beside her, suddenly shy in the presence of such finery.

"Of course." Holly's hand instinctively found Jimmy's shoulder, offering reassurance. "How may I help you?"

Miss Henley stepped forward, her grey eyes kind but serious. "We come bearing rather extraordinary news. A lady of considerable means has taken notice of your work with these children."

Holly's breath caught. She had dreamed of such possibilities during long nights on Copper Lane, imagining proper schoolrooms and warm meals for her little flock.

"This benefactress wishes to remain anonymous," Mrs Foster continued, "but her intentions are entirely genuine. She has inherited substantial wealth and seeks worthy causes for her philanthropy."

"She was orphaned herself at a young age," Miss Henley added gently. "Your situation and dedication have touched her heart deeply."

Holly felt Jim's grip tighten on her hand. Around them, other children had begun gathering—Maisie clutching her slate, Peter with ink-stained fingers from copying letters, Annie holding baby Tom's hand.

"What would she require of me?" Holly asked, though hope already bloomed in her chest like spring roses.

Mrs Foster withdrew a sealed envelope from her reticule. "A private consultation tomorrow evening. She wishes to discuss funding arrangements, proper facilities, perhaps even trained teachers to assist your efforts."

The words painted themselves across Holly's imagination— walls instead of alley corners, books instead of scratched slates, warm clothing instead of threadbare shawls. Her children deserved so much more than she could provide alone.

"The meeting location is contained within," Miss Henley said, indicating the envelope. "Six o'clock tomorrow evening."

Mrs Foster leaned closer, her voice dropping to a confidential whisper. "She asked us to tell you something specific, so you would know the sincerity of her offer." She paused dramatically. "Roses bloom brightest after harsh winters."

Holly's heart lurched. The phrase echoed her mother's final words, the promise that had sustained her through four years of hardship, on the streets and three in Hart House. Someone who understood that truth, who recognised the beauty that could emerge from suffering, surely possessed the wisdom to help these forgotten children.

"I'll be there," Holly said, accepting the envelope with trembling fingers. "Tomorrow evening."

The ladies exchanged satisfied glances before taking their leave. Jim tugged at Holly's sleeve as they watched the elegant figures disappear into the crowd.

"Miss Holly, what's a bene-fac-tress?"

"Someone who helps people, little one." Holly gazed down at the envelope, feeling its weight like a promise. "Someone who might help us build the school we've dreamed about."

Around her, the children erupted in excited chatter, their voices bright with possibility.

EVERYTHING CHANGES

*H*olly clutched the envelope against her chest as she hurried through the narrow streets toward Copper Lane, her heart racing with possibilities. The late afternoon shadows stretched long across the cobblestones, but for once the approaching darkness held no fear—only promise.

She found Nell and Benjamin waiting outside Mrs Farthings' boarding house, their faces expectant. Word travelled fast amongst the street children, and Holly's animated departure from the market had not gone unnoticed.

"Well?" Nell demanded, her dark eyes sparkling with curiosity. "Those fancy ladies looked important enough to own half of Ashford."

Holly laughed, the sound bubbling up from somewhere deep within her chest. "Oh, Nell! You won't believe it." She pressed the envelope to her heart again. "There's a benefactress—a wealthy lady who wants to fund our work with the children."

Benjamin leaned forward on his walking stick, eyebrows raised. "Fund? As in actual money?"

"Proper facilities," Holly breathed, the words tasting like honey on her tongue. "Books, slates, warm clothing. Maybe even trained teachers to help us." She spun in a small circle, her patched skirt swirling around her ankles. "Can you imagine? Real classrooms instead of alleyways and doorsteps."

Nell grabbed Holly's hands, joining in her excitement. "Maisie could have her own reading primer! And little Tom wouldn't have to share chalk with six other children."

"We could teach them proper penmanship," Benjamin added, his Welsh accent thick with emotion. "Give them skills that might lift them from these streets forever."

The three of them stood in the fading light, dreams weaving between them like golden threads. Holly pictured rows of clean wooden desks, shelves lined with books, windows that let in morning sunshine. She saw her children—her precious little flock—with full bellies and warm coats, their faces bright with learning instead of pinched with hunger.

"When's this meeting then?" Nell asked, her practical nature reasserting itself.

"Tomorrow evening at six." Holly's fingers traced the edges of the envelope. "The lady wishes to remain anonymous, but she was orphaned young herself. She understands what these children face."

Benjamin shifted his weight, concern flickering across his features. "Perhaps we should wait for Daniel. He's back from London tomorrow, isn't he? Might be wise to have him look over any arrangements before you—"

"Oh, Benjamin." Holly waved away his caution with a gesture that sent her auburn hair catching the last rays of sunlight. "This will be wonderful news to surprise him with when he returns. Can you imagine his face when I tell him we've secured funding?"

She pulled her worn Bible from her pocket, its leather cover soft from countless readings. Holding it close, Holly closed her eyes and whispered a prayer into the gathering dusk.

"If this funding is meant for good, surely God has a plan for us? He's brought us this far through every trial." Her voice grew stronger, filled with the same faith that had sustained her through Cordelia's cruelties and four years of street life. "Perhaps this is how the roses finally bloom again."

When she opened her eyes, both Nell and Benjamin were watching her with expressions of wonder. In the twilight, Holly's face seemed to glow with an inner light that transformed her worn features into something almost ethereal.

"Tomorrow evening," she said firmly, tucking the Bible back into her pocket. "Tomorrow evening, everything changes."

DARKNESS FALLS

*H*olly woke before dawn on the day of the meeting, her heart drumming against her ribs like a caged bird. She pressed her face to the small window of her lodging room, watching the first pale light creep across Ashford's rooftops. Today would change everything—she could feel it in her bones.

She pulled on her best dress, a faded blue cotton that had once belonged to her mother. Holly had mended it countless times, her careful stitches creating a patchwork of love across the worn fabric. The sleeves were too short now, revealing the sharp angles of her wrists, but it was clean and modest. She smoothed the skirt with trembling hands, pulling her shoulders back the way her mother had taught her years ago.

"A lady carries herself with dignity, no matter her circumstances," Mary's gentle voice whispered through memory.

Holly twisted her auburn hair into a simple knot, securing it with the last remaining pins from her mother's dressing table. In the cracked mirror above the washstand, she barely recognised the young woman staring back—thin but determined, her green eyes bright with possibility.

The morning crawled by with agonising slowness. Holly taught the children their letters, but her thoughts kept drifting to the evening ahead. Maisie noticed her distraction, tugging at Holly's skirt.

"Miss Holly, you look different today. All shiny."

"I feel shiny," Holly admitted, smoothing the child's tangled hair. "Tonight might bring wonderful changes for all of us."

As six o'clock approached, Holly made her way through the darkening streets, the envelope clutched in her gloved hand. The address led her to the better part of town, where gas lamps cast steady pools of light and the buildings stood tall and respectable.

But when Holly found the correct number, her footsteps faltered on the pavement. Before her loomed a grey stone building that resembled more fortress than charitable office. Narrow windows peered down like watchful eyes, and the heavy oak door bore a brass plate that made her stomach clench.

Dr Silas Creighton, Physician

Consultations by Appointment

Holly's breath caught in her throat. This was no benefactress's office—this was a doctor's surgery. The realisation crept up her spine like ice water, but she forced herself to step closer. Perhaps the benefactress worked with medical professionals? Orphaned children often needed health assessments before placement in schools.

The door opened at her tentative knock, and a thin man with calculating eyes beckoned her inside. The surgery's interior felt wrong—mismatched furniture arranged hastily, medical instruments gleaming coldly in the lamplight. Everything spoke of expedience rather than comfort.

"Miss Clarke, I presume?" Dr Creighton's voice carried an oily smoothness that made Holly's skin crawl.

But the children needed this opportunity. Holly lifted her chin and stepped across the threshold, even as every instinct screamed at her to run.

ENSNARED

$\mathcal{H}$olly stepped deeper into the surgery, her unease mounting with each echoing footfall on the cold stone floor. The lamplight flickered across surgical instruments that gleamed like teeth in the shadows, and the air carried the sharp bite of carbolic acid mixed with something darker—fear, perhaps, or desperation.

Dr Creighton's voice slithered through the silence. "Do come in. We've been expecting you."

The words struck Holly like a physical blow. But before she could retreat, a figure emerged from the shadows beyond the examination table—tall, elegant, and terrifyingly familiar.

Lady Cordelia Hart stood in the dimly lit room like a queen surveying her domain, her cold blue eyes fixed on Holly with predatory satisfaction. She wore a deep burgundy dress that seemed to absorb the lamplight, making her appear more shadow than substance. The years had sharpened her features into something aristocratic and cruel, her dark blonde hair swept into an elaborate coiffure that spoke of wealth and position.

"Holly Clarke." Cordelia's voice dripped with mockery, each

syllable carefully enunciated like drops of poison. "How unfortunate that grief over your parents' deaths has driven you quite mad."

Holly's breath caught in her throat. The careful composure she'd maintained for four years shattered like glass. "Aunt Cordelia? What are you—how did you—"

"Dr Creighton has examined you," Cordelia continued, ignoring Holly's stammered questions, "and determined you suffer from hysterical delusions. Claiming to be an heiress when you are clearly nothing but a disturbed beggar girl."

The coldness in Cordelia's voice cut through Holly's resolve like a blade through silk. Four years of survival, of building something meaningful from nothing, dismissed with casual cruelty. Holly felt herself shrinking beneath that pitiless gaze, becoming once again the frightened child who'd scrubbed floors until her hands bled.

"That's not true," Holly whispered, then found her voice. "I am Holly Clarke, daughter of Reverend Thomas Clarke and Mary Clarke of Roseworth Cottage. I am not mad."

Cordelia's laugh was sharp as breaking crystal. "Listen to her ravings, Doctor. She believes herself the daughter of a clergyman, heir to property she could never possess. Such delusions are common among the vagrant poor who've lost their wits to hardship."

Holly's chest tightened as the trap revealed itself in all its calculated malice. No benefactress. No opportunity for the children. Only Cordelia's web, spun with meticulous care to ensnare her.

"You killed your own cat," Holly said, desperation lending strength to her voice. "You tried to poison me that night. I saw it die in convulsions from the laudanum you put in my stew."

"More delusions." Cordelia examined her gloved fingers with affected boredom. "The poor creature speaks of dead cats and poisoned meals. Clearly, her mind has fractured completely."

201

As Holly opened her mouth to protest further, shadows moved behind Dr Creighton. Two burly attendants stepped forward like gargoyles come to life—broad-shouldered men with blank, unfeeling faces and hands like ham hocks. Their grey uniforms bore the institutional stamp of those who handled society's unwanted.

Holly's blood turned to ice water. "No. No, this is wrong. I'm not mad. I teach children. I have friends who will vouch for—"

The attendants seized her arms with practised efficiency, their grip firm as manacles. Holly struggled against their hold, her mother's mended dress tearing at the shoulder seam.

"Nell!" she called out desperately. "Benjamin! Someone help me!"

But the surgery's thick stone walls swallowed her cries. Beyond the narrow windows, Ashford continued its evening bustle, unaware that one of its own was being stolen away.

Cordelia watched Holly's struggles with frigid satisfaction, like a cat observing a trapped mouse. From her reticule, she withdrew a folded document bearing official seals and handed it to Dr Creighton.

"The committal order," she said with calculated calm. "Signed by my husband, Sir Geoffrey Hart, as concerned family requesting professional evaluation of Miss Eliza Smith—a vagrant girl of unsound mind found wandering our property."

Holly's heart hammered against her ribs. Even her name had been stolen, replaced with that of a convenient nobody. "My name is Holly Clarke! Check the parish records—my father was the rector at St Nicholas!"

"Poor thing," Cordelia murmured to Dr Creighton. "She's constructed an entire fantasy around this dead clergyman's family. Most tragic."

Dr Creighton's expression reflected profound ambition as he tucked the document into his waistcoat. Cordelia pressed a well-stuffed leather purse into his waiting palm, the coins within clinking with metallic promise.

"Take her to Blackstone Asylum," Cordelia commanded, her voice carrying the authority of unquestioned wealth. "I'm told patients rarely leave once properly ... settled."

The physician's smile was razor-thin. "Indeed, my lady. The institution provides excellent long-term care for those suffering such ... persistent delusions."

Holly's struggles intensified as the attendants began dragging her toward the door. "You can't do this! I'm not mad! Daniel will look for me—Sir Richard knows who I am!"

"More fantasies," Cordelia observed. "She claims acquaintance with the Thornhill family. Quite elaborate, these delusions."

The surgery's atmosphere thickened with tension, cold as the stone walls around them. Holly felt the weight of Cordelia's victory pressing down like a physical force. Four years of survival, of hope rebuilt from ashes, crumbling beneath her aunt's methodical cruelty.

As the attendants hauled her from Dr Creighton's surgery into the gaslit street, Holly caught one last glimpse of Cordelia's face—beautiful, pitiless, and utterly without mercy.

The trap had closed with surgical precision.

RACE AGAINST TIME

*S*omething had felt wrong from the moment Holly left for her meeting. Benjamin had lingered outside Mrs Farthings' boarding house after Holly departed, that familiar knot of unease twisting in his stomach—the same feeling that had kept him alive on these streets for years.

He'd followed at a distance, his clubfoot forcing him to work harder to keep pace through Ashford's winding lanes. Holly's excitement about the mysterious benefactress had been infectious, but Benjamin's instincts screamed caution. Wealthy ladies didn't usually seek out flower girls in back-alley surgeries.

Now, pressed against the shadowed doorway of a milliner's shop across from Dr Creighton's building, Benjamin watched his worst fears unfold. The black carriage waited like a hearse, its windows dark as coal. Two attendants in grey uniforms dragged Holly from the surgery entrance, her struggles violent but futile against their practised grip.

Benjamin's heart hammered against his ribs. Holly's torn dress caught the gaslight as she thrashed, her voice carrying desperate pleas across the narrow street. Behind her emerged a woman in expensive silk—tall, imperious, watching Holly's capture with cold satisfaction.

Lady Hart. Had to be. The resemblance to Holly's gentle features was there, but twisted into something cruel and calculating.

"To the Asylum with her!" The cruel looking woman ordered.

The attendants shoved Holly into the carriage's black interior. The door slammed shut with the finality of a coffin lid. Benjamin's protective instincts blazed to life—this was his family being stolen away, the girl who'd taught him that kindness could flourish even in the gutters.

The carriage lurched into motion, wheels clattering against cobblestones.

Benjamin pushed off from the doorway and ran.

His clubfoot sent jolts of pain up his leg with each stride, but he ignored the familiar ache. The crowded evening streets blurred past—vendors hawking their final wares, elegantly dressed ladies examining shop windows, gentlemen in top hats discussing business. Benjamin dodged between them all, his breath coming in ragged gasps.

A stack of wooden crates blocked his path. Benjamin leaped over them, landing hard on his good foot and stumbling forward. Pain shot through his ankle, but he pressed on. Holly needed him.

Daniel's office lay six streets away, past the cathedral spire and through the legal district. Benjamin had memorised every shortcut during their months of friendship. He cut through the narrow passage behind the baker's shop, vaulted a low stone wall, and emerged onto High Street.

His lungs burned. Sweat stung his eyes. But Benjamin ran harder, determination driving him forward with each uneven step. The town transformed into a streaming blur of gaslight and shadow as he raced against time, praying Daniel had returned from London.

Holly had saved them all. Now it was his turn to save her.

SCREAMS

$\mathcal{T}$he carriage lurched forward, wheels grinding against cobblestones with merciless rhythm. Holly threw herself against the door, but the attendants' iron grips held her fast.

"Help me!" Her voice tore from her throat, raw and desperate. "Please, someone help me!"

The sounds of Ashford's evening bustle filtered through the carriage walls—vendors calling their final wares, ladies chattering about their purchases, gentlemen discussing business affairs. Holly's screams pierced the ordinary symphony of town life, but the world remained cruelly indifferent. Pedestrians continued their conversations, absorbed in their own concerns. A mother pulled her curious child closer when he turned toward the black carriage, but she didn't pause to investigate the frantic cries echoing from within.

"They're taking me against my will!" Holly's voice cracked with desperation. "I'm Holly Clarke—please!"

But the carriage rolled on, carrying her away from everything she'd fought to build. The attendants stared ahead with practiced indifference, as if they'd heard countless similar pleas echo within these dark walls.

Holly's struggles weakened as exhaustion claimed her limbs. She closed her eyes, feeling the familiar weight of her father's Bible pressed against her chest beneath her bodice. The words came like breathing, born from years of seeking comfort in prayer.

"Please, God, I've survived so much; surely You have not brought me this far to abandon me now."

The carriage swayed around a corner, and Holly's thoughts flickered to Daniel. His gentle smile when he'd first recognised her in the market. The warmth in his dark brown eyes as he'd read stories to the children. The way he'd stepped back so carefully when she'd pulled away from their almost-kiss, placing her comfort above his own desires.

She'd been such a fool. All those careful walls she'd built around her heart, all that fear of trusting completely. Daniel had shown her nothing but kindness, had promised to help her reclaim Roseworth, had supported her work with the children without expecting anything in return.

Her chest tightened with regret sharp as any physical pain. She should have told him. Should have looked into those warm brown eyes and spoken the truth that had been growing in her heart for months—that somewhere between his patient visits and gentle encouragement, she'd fallen completely in love with him.

Now she might never get the chance.

The carriage wheels drummed their relentless rhythm, carrying her toward Blackstone Asylum and away from everything she'd dared to hope for.

SPEED

*D*aniel pushed open the freshly painted door of his office, satisfaction warming his chest as he stepped inside. The legal documents spread across his mahogany desk represented months of meticulous work—witness statements, financial records, forged signatures, all compiled into an iron-clad case that would see Cordelia Hart face justice at last. The court request sat, ready for submission in his waist-coat pocket: every detail verified and cross-referenced. After four years of believing Holly dead, he finally possessed the power to restore her inheritance and expose Cordelia's crimes.

The relief of returning from London still coursed through him. Tomorrow, he would present the evidence to the magistrate. Tomorrow, everything would change.

Heavy footsteps thundered up the stairs outside his office. Daniel frowned, recognising the uneven gait—Benjamin's distinctive rhythm, made urgent by desperation. The door burst open without ceremony.

Benjamin stumbled across the threshold, sweat streaming down his face and soaking through his patched shirt. His chest heaved as he fought for breath, one hand clutching the door-frame for support whilst his clubfoot dragged behind him.

"Mr Thornhill!" Benjamin's voice cracked with exhaustion and terror. "You must come quickly! It's Holly—she's in danger!"

Daniel's satisfaction evaporated like morning mist. The carefully organised papers on his desk suddenly meant nothing compared to the panic blazing in Benjamin's eyes. His heart hammered against his ribs as fragments of worry—Holly's recent unease about being watched, her fears about Cordelia's reach—crashed together in his mind.

"What do you mean? Where is she?" Daniel demanded, already moving toward his coat hanging on the wall peg. Benjamin's distress sent ice through his veins. Holly's face flashed before him—her gentle smile when teaching the children, the way her eyes lit up when she spoke of her dreams for a proper school, the courage that had carried her through four years on the streets.

"I followed her to that meeting," Benjamin gasped, still struggling to catch his breath. "With the benefactress—it was a trap! Lady Hart was there, and two men in grey uniforms dragged her into a black carriage. They're taking her to the asylum!"

Daniel's face drained of colour as the full horror of the situation crystallised. Blackstone Asylum—that grey stone fortress on Ashford's outskirts where patients disappeared forever into a system designed to forget them. He'd heard whispers about Dr Creighton's willingness to sign committal papers for the right price, about the asylum's reputation for breaking spirits along with minds.

"God help us ..." Daniel breathed, grabbing his black coat and thrusting his arms through the sleeves. The legal case on his desk could wait—Holly couldn't. Every second of delay meant the carriage carried her further from safety, closer to the living death Cordelia had planned.

"How long ago?" Daniel's voice rang with authority as he

fastened his coat, his mind already calculating distances and travel times.

"Perhaps ten minutes. I ran as fast as I could—"

Daniel clasped Benjamin's shoulder firmly. "You did exactly right. Thank you."

Without another moment's hesitation, Daniel bolted from the office, his polished boots pounding down the wooden stairs and out into the cobblestone street. The evening air hit his face as he sprinted toward the stable behind his building, his heart hammering with desperate urgency.

The stable boy looked up in surprise as Daniel burst through the doors. "Saddle Perseus immediately!" Daniel commanded, referring to his black stallion—a powerful beast bred for speed and endurance.

Within moments, the magnificent horse stood ready, his dark coat gleaming and muscles taut with contained energy. Daniel swung into the saddle with practiced ease, gathering the reins in steady hands despite the chaos in his chest.

"Hyah!" Daniel spurred Perseus forward, and the stallion leaped into motion with explosive power. Hooves clattered against cobblestones as they burst from the stable yard onto the main thoroughfare, weaving between evening traffic with reckless determination.

The sounds of Ashford blurred past—vendors calling final sales, carriage wheels rumbling over stone, children playing in doorways. Daniel's world had narrowed to a single focus: reaching Holly before Cordelia's trap closed completely around her.

Perseus's powerful stride ate up the distance, his breathing steady and strong as they navigated the winding streets leading toward the north road. Daniel leaned low over the stallion's neck, urging every ounce of speed from the magnificent animal.

Holly's face filled his mind—her quiet strength, her unwavering faith, the way she'd transformed a cramped lodging room into a sanctuary for lost children. The thought of her trapped in that black carriage, terrified and alone, drove him forward with desperate purpose.

The city's edge approached rapidly, buildings giving way to countryside where a single road led toward Blackstone's forbidding walls. Daniel's jaw set with grim determination as Perseus's hooves thundered against the packed earth.

He would reach her. He had to.

REACH OF SALVATION

*P*erseus's hooves drummed against the cobblestones like thunder as Daniel navigated through the evening crowds. His mind raced faster than his stallion's gallop, fragments of desperate prayers tumbling through his thoughts with each jarring stride.

Lord, guide my way. Let me reach her in time. Give me strength, give me speed, give me wisdom.

The reins felt slick in his sweating palms as he urged Perseus around a slow-moving cart laden with turnips, the stallion's powerful muscles bunching and releasing beneath him. Evening shoppers scattered from their path, some shouting complaints that Daniel couldn't hear above the roar of blood in his ears.

Please, God, don't let me be too late. Holly has suffered enough.

A group of children playing hoops in the street looked up with wide eyes as the black stallion thundered past, Perseus's nostrils flaring with exertion. Daniel leaned lower over the horse's neck, feeling the animal's heart hammering against his legs as they pushed toward the city's northern edge.

The streets grew narrower as he approached Ashford's outskirts, terraced houses giving way to scattered cottages and finally open countryside. Daniel's chest burned with each breath, but his resolve crystallised with every passing moment. Holly's gentle face filled his vision—the way she'd looked when teaching little Maisie to read, her quiet strength when speaking of her parents, the trust in her green eyes when she'd finally allowed herself to hope.

I will not fail her. Not again.

The main road stretched ahead like a grey ribbon cutting through the darkening landscape. Daniel's heart lurched as he spotted the black carriage perhaps two hundred yards ahead, its rectangular frame stark against the pale sky. The vehicle moved with inexorable purpose toward the looming silhouette on the horizon—Blackstone Asylum's forbidding walls.

Perseus responded to Daniel's urgent spurs with a burst of speed that pressed Daniel back in his saddle. The stallion's stride lengthened, hooves pounding against the packed earth with mechanical precision. The gap between them and the carriage began to close.

The asylum's grey stone walls grew larger with each passing moment, their surface pitted and stained by decades of rain and neglect. Barred windows stared down like dead eyes, whilst the iron gates ahead promised finality. Once those gates closed behind Holly, retrieving her would require navigating a labyrinth of corrupt officials and forged documents.

Not while I draw breath.

Daniel's voice rang out across the countryside as he drew closer to the carriage. "Stop! In the name of the Crown, I command you to stop!"

The driver—a scruffy figure in a threadbare coat—glanced back briefly before flicking his reins with deliberate indifference. The carriage horses picked up their pace slightly, but their steady trot remained no match for Perseus's thundering gallop.

"Stop this instant!" Daniel shouted again, his barrister's

training lending authority to his voice that had swayed court-rooms and cowed hardened criminals.

But the driver showed no intention of compliance, hunched over his reins as the asylum gates loomed ever closer. Daniel could make out the dark shape of a gatehouse, light flickering in its windows as evening settled over the countryside.

Time stretched and compressed around him as possibilities flashed through his mind. He could follow them through the gates, but that would mean confronting armed guards and navigating bureaucratic obstacles whilst Holly disappeared into the asylum's depths. He could ride back to fetch Sir Richard, but precious minutes would slip away—minutes Holly might not have.

The carriage was less than fifty yards ahead now, close enough for Daniel to see the iron reinforcements on its doors, the barred windows that proclaimed its grim purpose. Somewhere inside that rolling prison, Holly sat trapped and terrified, probably wondering if anyone would come for her.

I'm coming, Holly. Hold on.

Perseus's breathing remained strong and steady despite their breakneck pace, the magnificent animal responding to Daniel's urgency with everything in his powerful frame. The distance closed to thirty yards, then twenty, the sound of the carriage wheels and horses' hooves mingling with Perseus's thundering stride.

Daniel's mind calculated distances and angles with the precision that had served him well in Cambridge mathematics. The carriage driver sat exposed on his perch, the vehicle's momentum carrying it forward in a predictable line. If Daniel could reach him ...

This is madness. The rational part of his mind catalogued the risks—a fall at this speed could break bones or worse, the driver might be armed, the carriage could overturn with Holly inside.

But rationality crumbled before the image of Holly's trusting face, before the memory of her quiet courage in the face of years of suffering.

With a surge of desperate determination, Daniel urged Perseus alongside the carriage. The stallion responded magnificently, his powerful stride eating up the final yards until they ran parallel with the black vehicle. The asylum gates were less than a hundred yards ahead now, their iron bars promising imprisonment and despair.

The driver looked over in alarm, his weathered face creased with surprise and growing concern. He raised his whip as if to strike at Daniel, but the barrister was already moving.

For Holly.

Daniel released his grip on the reins and launched himself from Perseus's back toward the carriage. For a terrifying moment he hung suspended in the air between horse and vehicle, the ground rushing past beneath him in a blur of grey stone and brown earth.

His hands found purchase on the carriage's iron rail, his body slamming against the vehicle's side with jarring force. The driver cursed and reached for his whip, but Daniel was already hauling himself upward with strength born of desperation.

"What are you—" the driver snarled, but his protest cut short as Daniel seized the reins with one hand whilst gripping the man's coat with the other.

The carriage lurched as Daniel wrestled for control, the horses snorting in confusion as their steady rhythm faltered. The driver struggled against Daniel's grip, his elbow catching the barrister in the ribs, but Daniel held on with desperate tenacity.

The asylum gates loomed directly ahead now, perhaps thirty yards away. Daniel could see movement in the gatehouse as guards prepared to admit their expected cargo.

With a final surge of strength, Daniel wrenched the reins hard to the left whilst shoving the driver aside. The carriage horses responded to the sudden command, their hooves skidding on the packed earth as the vehicle slewed sideways and ground to a shuddering halt.

Daniel leaped down from the driver's perch, his heart hammering as he reached for the carriage door handle. His hands shook as he gripped the iron latch, knowing Holly waited inside—alive, terrified, but within reach of salvation.

The door swung open.

SAFETY

*H*olly pressed herself against the far corner of the carriage, her fingers digging into the worn leather seat as the vehicle lurched to a sudden halt. The iron latch rattled, and terror seized her throat—had they reached the asylum already? Were those grey-uniformed guards coming to drag her inside?

But the voice that rang out through the evening air made her heart leap with impossible hope.

"Release her!"

Daniel. The name burst through her mind like sunlight breaking through storm clouds. She knew that voice, had dreamed of it during countless cold nights on the streets, had listened to it reading stories to children by candlelight. Holly's eyes flew to the carriage door as it swung open, revealing Daniel's familiar face etched with fierce determination.

He was here. Against all odds, despite the careful trap Cordelia had laid, Daniel had found her.

The attendants' grip on her arms tightened reflexively, their beefy fingers pressing cruelly into her flesh. The larger of the two men leaned forward, his scarred face twisting into a sneer of professional disdain.

"We have papers," he growled, brandishing the folded committal order like a weapon. The parchment crackled as he waved it, the forged signatures catching the fading light. "Legal committal, signed proper-like. This girl's mad as a March hare, claiming to be some toff's daughter when she's nothing but a beggar off the streets."

Holly opened her mouth to protest, but Daniel's voice cut through the air with unwavering authority.

"Forged papers," he stated, his barrister's training evident in every syllable. No tremor of doubt weakened his words, no uncertainty clouded his purpose. "This is Holly Clarke, legal heir to the Roseworth estate."

The second attendant shifted uncomfortably, his weathered hands loosening slightly on Holly's arm. She felt the change immediately—the first crack in their certainty, the beginning of doubt that Daniel's presence had introduced into their simple transaction.

Daniel reached into his waist-coat pocket and withdrew a folded document, holding it with the same confidence he might display before a judge's bench. "There is a warrant being issued even now for the arrest of Lady Cordelia Hart for fraud and attempted murder."

Holly's breath caught. A warrant? Her mind reeled as the implications crashed over her like waves against a cliff. All these years of fear, all the nights spent wondering if Cordelia would find her, and now—

"Any man who touches Miss Clarke from this moment forward," Daniel continued, his voice carrying the weight of legal consequence, "will be charged as an accomplice."

The change in the carriage was immediate and electric. The larger attendant's grip faltered, his scarred face cycling through confusion, calculation, and growing unease. Holly could practically see him weighing his options—the coins Cordelia had promised against the very real threat of a magistrate's justice.

The second man was already releasing her arm, stepping back as far as the cramped carriage would allow. "I don't know nothing about no murders," he muttered, his voice thick with sudden nervousness. "Just doing a job, taking a sick girl to proper care."

"Shut your mouth," the first attendant snapped, but his own confidence was crumbling. Holly could see it in the way his eyes darted between Daniel's resolute face and the legal document in his hand, in the subtle loosening of his grip on her other arm.

Holly's heart hammered against her ribs as the tension stretched taut in the small space. Everything balanced on this moment—her freedom, her future, perhaps her very life. The asylum gates loomed somewhere behind Daniel, their iron bars waiting to swallow her whole if these men chose to complete their grim task.

But doubt had taken root now, and it spread like cracks through their resolve. The larger attendant's face showed the same uncertainty Holly had seen in countless street children when confronted with authority they couldn't challenge or intimidate.

"Legal heir, you say?" The second man's voice wavered. "With papers and all?"

"Proper papers," Daniel confirmed, never breaking eye contact with Holly. In his gaze she saw everything she had longed to believe—safety, protection, love that would brave any danger to reach her.

With visible reluctance, the first attendant released his grip on Holly's arm. She stumbled forward immediately, her legs unsteady after the terror of the past hour, her body trembling with the aftershock of fear and the overwhelming relief of rescue.

Daniel caught her before she could fall, his strong arms

enveloping her in an embrace that felt like coming home after years of wandering. Holly pressed her face against his chest, breathing in the familiar scent of books and ink that always clung to his clothes, feeling the steady rhythm of his heartbeat beneath her cheek.

"I have you," Daniel whispered, his voice rough with emotion. One hand cupped the back of her head whilst the other held her securely against him, as if he could shield her from every cruel thing the world might attempt.

Holly's composure finally cracked, months of careful control dissolving as tears spilled down her cheeks. She was safe. After all the years of looking over her shoulder, all the nights of wondering when Cordelia's reach might find her again, she was finally, truly safe.

"You're safe now," Daniel murmured against her hair, his words a sacred promise. "I promise you're safe."

Holly closed her eyes and let herself believe it.

STATEMENTS AT THE COURT

*H*olly sat in the front row of Ashford's courthouse, her hands folded tightly in her lap as she watched Cordelia Hart enter flanked by two uniformed officers. The woman who had once terrorised her with calculated cruelty now appeared diminished—her face ashen, her once-immaculate hair dishevelled, her expensive silk gown wrinkled from a night in a cell.

Yet even in defeat, Cordelia's eyes burned with fury as they swept across the packed courtroom. When her gaze found Holly, something twisted and vindictive flickered there, as if she blamed Holly for her own downfall rather than acknowledging the consequences of her actions.

The courtroom buzzed with whispers and shuffling feet. Holly had never seen so many people crammed into one space—farmers and shopkeepers, ladies in their finest bonnets, gentlemen with pocket watches, all drawn by the scandalous tale of a lady's fall from grace. The air thrummed with anticipation, thick enough to taste.

Daniel stood at the prosecution table, a collection of documents spread before him like weapons prepared for battle. His face bore the gravity of the moment, but when he glanced at Holly, she saw the fierce protectiveness that had driven him to build this case stone by stone.

"The prosecution calls Mrs Miriam Dawes," the clerk announced, though everyone knew the elderly cook would not be taking the stand herself.

Daniel rose, holding a sealed envelope with hands that trembled slightly. "Your Honour, Mrs Dawes has sadly passed away, but not before providing this sworn statement regarding the events at Hart House."

Holly's throat tightened as Daniel broke the seal and unfolded the letter. Mrs Dawes had been one of the few kind souls at Hart House, and now her final act would speak for all those who had suffered under Cordelia's roof.

Daniel's voice carried across the hushed courtroom as he read the damning confession. "On the evening of November fifteenth, I witnessed Lady Cordelia Hart adding drops from a brown laudanum bottle to Miss Holly Clarke's dinner bowl. When I attempted to warn the child, Lady Hart's Persian cat consumed the poisoned meal and died in violent convulsions."

Gasps rippled through the gallery. Holly closed her eyes, remembering that terrible night—the cat's agonised writhing, the way Cordelia's mask had slipped to reveal cold satisfaction beneath the feigned concern.

"I have carried this knowledge like a stone in my chest," Daniel continued reading. "I should have spoken sooner. I should have protected that innocent child. May God forgive my cowardice, and may this testimony serve justice at last."

Holly wiped away tears as murmurs swept the courtroom. Beside her, she heard a woman whisper, "Poisoning her own niece! What manner of creature—"

Daniel presented document after document with methodical precision. The forged signatures on withdrawal vouchers, showing how Cordelia had embezzled from Holly's trust whilst claiming the girl was dead. The fraudulent guardian fees collected for years after Holly's supposed death. The timeline of "accidents"—loose stones, frayed ropes, dangerous errands—all carefully orchestrated to appear coincidental.

Then the servants testified. Mary the scullery maid spoke of the stone deliberately loosened on the kitchen steps. The groundskeeper described the well rope he'd been ordered not to repair despite its obvious deterioration. Each testimony built upon the last, constructing an unshakeable foundation of premeditated cruelty.

The courthouse doors creaked open, and Holly turned to see Sir Geoffrey Hart shuffle in, flanked by constables. The man who had once commanded respect as a gentleman now appeared broken—his shoulders stooped, his face grey with exhaustion and guilt. When he took the witness stand, his hands shook so violently he could barely place them on the Bible.

"State your name for the record," the clerk instructed.

"Sir Geoffrey ... Geoffrey Hart." His voice cracked.

Daniel approached with gentle authority. "Sir Geoffrey, please tell the court about your wife's treatment of Miss Holly Clarke."

Geoffrey's composure crumbled entirely. "She ... Cordelia manipulated me. Made me believe Holly was ungrateful, troublesome. But the truth ..." He buried his face in his hands. "The truth is my wife celebrated when she thought the child was dead. She said our problems were solved, that we could finally claim what was rightfully ours."

The courtroom erupted in shocked murmurs. Holly felt sick remembering Geoffrey's weak protests, his brandy-soaked compliance with Cordelia's schemes.

"She convinced me it was justice," Geoffrey continued through his tears. "Said Mary had stolen Cordelia's inheritance, that we deserved compensation. But watching that child suffer

..." His voice broke completely. "I am as guilty as she for every cruel day."

When court recessed, Holly stepped outside for air, overwhelmed by the magnitude of testimony. The courthouse steps teemed with spectators discussing the revelations in hushed, scandalised tones.

"Never heard the like of it," an elderly man muttered to his companion. "A lady of quality attempting murder for money."

"Shows you can't trust anyone these days," replied a woman in a blue bonnet. "Poor little mite, what she must have endured."

JUSTICE

The trial had become the sensation of the county. Holly spotted familiar faces from villages miles away, all drawn by the shocking tale of betrayal and attempted murder in Ashford's highest circles. Scribes scribbled furiously, capturing every detail for newspapers that would carry the story across England.

When court reconvened, Holly watched Dr Silas Creighton take the stand, his oily demeanour replaced by nervous perspiration. The unscrupulous physician's role in Cordelia's plot unravelled quickly under questioning—his willingness to sign false committal papers, his ready participation in what amounted to kidnapping.

"The defendant approached me with a proposition," Dr Creighton admitted reluctantly. "A fee for professional services regarding a ... difficult family matter."

"You mean conspiring to have an innocent woman committed to an asylum," Daniel pressed.

"I was assured she required care," Dr Creighton protested weakly, but his excuses fooled no one.

Holly shuddered remembering his cold surgery, the trap Cordelia had set with such calculating precision.

As evidence mounted against her, Cordelia's composure began fracturing visibly. Holly watched her aunt's face cycle through disbelief, rage, and something approaching madness. During breaks, constables reported that Cordelia spent hours in her cell scrubbing her hands raw whilst muttering incoherently.

"Roses and ashes," one officer whispered to his colleague. "Keeps saying something about a girl with green eyes watching her."

The final day arrived with thunderous anticipation. The judge, his face grave with the weight of justice, rose to address the packed courtroom.

"Lady Cordelia Hart," he pronounced with solemn authority, "you have been found guilty of fraud, attempted murder, and conspiracy to commit unlawful imprisonment."

The courthouse held its breath.

"You are hereby sentenced to life imprisonment, to be served in Her Majesty's Prison. Furthermore, Miss Holly Clarke's trust shall be repaid in full and restored to its proper amount. Should you lack sufficient funds, your belongings shall be sold to meet this debt."

The gallery erupted. Holly felt Daniel's hand find hers as Cordelia's sentence echoed through the chamber like a funeral bell. Justice had arrived at last, but Holly found no joy in it—only relief that the nightmare was finally ending.

"Sir Geoffrey Hart," the judge continued, "your complicity earns you ten years' imprisonment."

Geoffrey nodded numbly, accepting his fate with the resignation of a man who had lost everything that mattered.

As constables led the condemned away, Holly rose from her seat, feeling the weight of four years' fear lifting from her shoulders. The girl who had fled Hart House in terror was gone, replaced by a young woman who had faced her demons and emerged victorious.

The courthouse emptied slowly, spectators discussing the shocking conclusion in taverns and parlours across Ashford. Holly knew this trial would reshape how people viewed authority and privilege, serving as a reminder that true nobility lay in character, not birth.

Outside, the afternoon sun felt warm on her face as she stood beside Daniel, finally free to build the future she had dreamed of during her darkest hours.

There was only one last thing to do …

REGRETS

The corridors of Ashford jail stretched before Holly like a grey tunnel, each footstep echoing against stone walls that had witnessed countless stories of justice and regret. Gas lamps flickered weakly in their brackets, casting dancing shadows that reminded her of the candlelit evenings in her cramped room on Copper Lane. Daniel walked beside her, his presence a steady anchor as they approached the chamber where Geoffrey Hart awaited.

The heavy door creaked open to reveal a sparse room furnished with nothing more than a wooden table and two chairs. Her uncle sat hunched forward, his hands clasped before him, no longer the gentleman who had once commanded respect at Hart House dinner parties. His dark brown hair, now completely grey at the temples, hung limp around a face marked by sleepless nights and bitter reflection.

Holly stepped across the threshold, her breath catching as she took in her uncle's transformed appearance. The portly figure she remembered had withered, his clothes hanging loose on a frame diminished by months of guilt and poor appetite.

When he raised his head, those light grey eyes that had once avoided difficult truths now held the raw honesty of a man who had lost everything.

"Holly." Geoffrey's voice emerged as barely more than a whisper, shaking with an emotion she had never heard from him before. The single word carried the weight of years—regret, shame, and something that might have been relief at finally facing her.

She studied his face, searching for traces of the man who had sat silently whilst Cordelia orchestrated her torment. How could this broken figure be the same person who had watched her scrub floors until her hands bled, who had turned away when she carried buckets too heavy for a child's arms?

"I am so sorry for what you've endured," Geoffrey continued, each word dragged from somewhere deep within his chest. "I failed you in every way that mattered. I was your guardian, your family, and I became your enemy through my own cowardice."

The sincerity in his voice cut through Holly's carefully constructed defences. She had prepared herself for this moment, rehearsing words of forgiveness during the carriage ride, but seeing him reduced to this shell of a man stirred unexpected compassion within her heart.

"You were afraid," Holly said quietly, her voice carrying no accusation, only understanding born from her own years of fear. "Fear makes people do terrible things, Uncle Geoffrey. I learned that lesson well enough."

Geoffrey's shoulders shook as he absorbed her words. "Fear, yes. But that's no excuse for what I allowed to happen. When I think of you as a child, carrying those heavy buckets, sleeping in that wretched little room ..." His voice broke entirely, and he buried his face in his hands.

Holly moved closer, her steps measured and deliberate. The man before her bore little resemblance to the Geoffrey who had nervously deferred to Cordelia's every whim, who had drowned his conscience in brandy rather than protect an innocent child. This was simply a human being drowning in remorse.

She took a deep breath, drawing strength from the roses her mother had taught her to tend, from the scripture her father had read by firelight, from the children she had sheltered on Copper Lane. Her voice, when it came, held the authority of someone who had walked through fire and emerged whole.

"You still have a chance to seek redemption, Uncle Geoffrey," she said softly, her green eyes meeting his grey ones directly. "The choices you make from this moment forward matter more than the mistakes behind you."

Without hesitation, Holly reached out and placed her hand gently on his shoulder. The gesture, so simple yet profound, bridged the chasm of pain that had separated them. Her touch carried forgiveness, not the bitter triumph of a victim over her oppressor, but the grace of someone who understood that healing required mercy.

"I forgive you," she continued, her words falling into the silence like stones dropped into still water. "You will always remain in my prayers, and I hope you find peace in your heart."

Geoffrey's eyes welled with tears that had been building for months, perhaps years. When he spoke, his voice carried a thickness that suggested he hadn't wept since childhood.

"Thank you, my dear," he whispered, the endearment emerging naturally, without calculation or manipulation. "You've always been the light of your parents' legacy. Thomas and Mary would be so proud of the woman you've become."

Holly felt her own eyes moisten at the mention of her parents. In Geoffrey's broken acknowledgement, she heard an echo of the love that had once filled Roseworth Cottage, the faith that had sustained her through the darkest nights.

Geoffrey straightened slightly, and Holly glimpsed something she had never seen in him before—genuine resolve. The weak man who had bent to Cordelia's will was gone, replaced by someone who finally understood the cost of his choices.

"I will do what's right from here on," he said, his voice growing stronger with each word. "I promise you that, Holly. I promise your parents that."

STEADY AND SURE

*T*he stone corridors of Ashford jail seemed to press closer as Holly made her way toward the women's wing, each footstep echoing with finality. The oppressive atmosphere grew thicker with every turn, heavy with despair and the accumulated weight of broken lives. Unlike Geoffrey's cell, which had felt sad but somehow hopeful, this section of the prison carried a different energy entirely—one that spoke of souls who had surrendered to darkness.

Holly paused before the heavy wooden door marked with Cordelia's name, her hand trembling slightly as she reached for the iron handle. Through the small barred window, she could see a figure hunched on the narrow bed, and for a moment, Holly almost didn't recognise the woman within.

Gone was the imperious Lady Cordelia Hart who had swept down the staircase of Hart House in silk and pearls. The woman who looked up as Holly entered bore little resemblance to the elegant socialite who had once commanded drawing rooms and manipulated charity committees. Her dark blonde hair hung lank and unwashed around gaunt cheeks, and the expensive gowns had been replaced by rough prison garb. Most striking of all, her cold blue eyes—once so calculating and controlled—now burned with a wild mixture of fury and desperation.

Cordelia clutched a grey shawl around her shoulders, the coarse wool a pitiful substitute for the cashmere and silk that had once adorned her frame. The gesture spoke of fallen grace more eloquently than any words could, this woman who had valued appearances above all else now reduced to clinging to scraps for warmth.

"You dare come here?" Cordelia's voice cracked like a whip through the small cell, her words sharp with venom. She rose from the bed with jerky, unsteady movements, her eyes never leaving Holly's face. "You think you can come and gloat over what you've done to me?"

Holly remained in the doorway, her gaze steady and calm despite the hatred radiating from her aunt. She had expected this reception, had prepared herself for Cordelia's rage, but seeing it manifest so rawly still sent a chill through her heart.

"I have not come to gloat, Aunt," Holly replied, her voice firm yet soft, carrying the strength she had learned on the streets and the grace her parents had instilled in her. "I came to say goodbye."

Cordelia's laugh was bitter and harsh, scraping against the stone walls like nails on slate. "Goodbye? How perfectly noble of you, playing the gracious martyr. But don't pretend this visit is anything other than triumph."

The accusation hung in the stale air between them, but Holly didn't flinch. She had learned to recognise poison when she heard it, had developed immunity to cruelty through years of surviving it.

"You'll never understand what you've cost me," Cordelia continued, her voice rising to a near shriek. "Everything I worked for, everything I deserved—gone because of you. You're nothing but a beggar girl who got lucky, and you've destroyed a woman of true quality."

Even now, stripped of everything, Cordelia clung to her delusions of superiority. Holly felt a stab of pity pierce through her defences as she recognised the profound emptiness that drove her aunt's desperate need to feel better than others.

"I understand more than you think," Holly said quietly, taking a careful step into the cell. The space felt smaller with both of them in it, cramped and suffocating. "I know what it means to lose everything, to feel forgotten and abandoned."

"Don't you dare compare us!" Cordelia spat, her fingers tightening convulsively on the shawl. "You were nothing to begin with. I had position, respect, a place in society that you could never comprehend."

Holly absorbed the words without letting them penetrate her heart. She had learned the difference between truth and the desperate lashing out of a wounded soul.

"I hope you can find peace, Aunt Cordelia," Holly said with genuine sincerity, moving closer despite the fury crackling in the air around her aunt. "Whatever drove you to such darkness, I hope you can find your way back to the light."

The words seemed to strike Cordelia like a physical blow. Her mouth opened and closed soundlessly for a moment before she found her voice again.

"Peace?" she hissed, but Holly caught the tremor of uncertainty beneath the bravado. "No one will ever forgive me for what I've done. There is no peace for someone like me."

"There could be," Holly said softly. "If you choose it."

For just an instant, something flickered across Cordelia's face—a crack in the armour of rage and bitterness. It was gone so quickly Holly almost missed it, but she had seen it: a glimpse of the lost soul beneath all the hatred.

Holly stepped back into the doorway, knowing her time here was finished. At the threshold, she took one final look at the woman who had shaped so much of her suffering. Cordelia sat on the edge of the bed now, the shawl wrapped tightly around her like armour against a world that no longer had a place for her.

"I hope the roses bloom for you again one day," Holly whispered, her mother's cherished words carrying across the small space like a benediction. The phrase hung in the air between them, a flicker of hope offered to someone who had forgotten such things existed.

Cordelia's head snapped up at the words, her eyes wide and startled, but Holly was already stepping through the doorway. She walked down the corridor without looking back, as the guard slammed the door shut. Her footsteps were steady and sure, carrying her away from the darkness of the past and toward the light of her future.

Daniel waited outside, his face anxious until he saw her emerge. Holly walked into his arms with renewed purpose flowing through her veins, ready to honour her parents' memory by building something beautiful from the ashes of her pain.

ROSEWORTH RESTORED

*T*he carriage wheels crunched over the familiar gravel path, and Holly's breath caught in her throat as Roseworth Cottage came into view. Seven years had passed since she'd left this place as a frightened ten-year-old, yet the sight of the weathered stone walls and slate roof sent memories flooding through her like a dam bursting.

Daniel's hand found hers in the carriage, his fingers warm and steady. "Are you ready?"

Holly nodded, though her throat felt too tight for words. Sir Richard had completed the legal proceedings that morning, officially recognising her as the rightful heir with Daniel's father serving as her temporary guardian until her twenty-first birthday. The papers in her reticule made it real, but seeing the cottage itself made her heart race with emotions too complex to name.

The carriage stopped, and Daniel stepped down first, extending his hand to help her descend. Holly's boots touched the familiar stones of the courtyard, and she had to steady herself against the carriage door as the full weight of homecoming settled over her.

"Your mother's roses," Daniel said softly, his voice filled with wonder. "They're still here, Holly. Wild and tangled, but alive."

Holly turned toward the garden and gasped. What had once been her mother's carefully tended paradise had transformed into something altogether different—a wilderness of thorns and blooms that defied every principle of proper gardening. The roses had grown unchecked, climbing over arbours that sagged under their weight, threading through broken trellises, and sprawling across pathways in glorious abandon. Yet they bloomed. Pink damask roses cascaded over the garden wall, white climbing roses had claimed the cottage's eastern wall, and deep red roses burst from tangles of green that reached nearly to her waist.

"Even in ashes, they bloom again," Holly whispered, her mother's final words returning to her with startling clarity.

She walked toward the garden as if in a trance, pushing through the overgrown gate that hung askew on rusted hinges. The sweet fragrance of roses filled the air, stronger and wilder than she remembered from childhood. Tears began streaming down her face before she realised she was crying—not from sadness, but from something deeper and more complicated. Relief. Gratitude. A sense of completion she hadn't known she'd been seeking.

Daniel followed at a respectful distance as Holly made her way through the tangled pathways, her dress catching on thorns that seemed determined to hold her back. She didn't care. Each step felt like reclaiming a piece of herself that had been lost for seven years.

At the garden's heart, she found what she'd been seeking without realising it. The small family plot lay partly hidden beneath trailing vines, but the simple stone markers remained visible. Her mother's grave, her father's beside it, exactly as she remembered from that terrible day when she'd watched the earth cover her last remaining parent.

Holly sank to her knees between the graves, her hands automatically beginning to clear the weeds that had grown over the stones. The marble felt cool beneath her palms as she traced the familiar engravings: "Mary Clarke, Beloved Wife and Mother" and "Thomas Clarke, Faithful Servant of God."

"Thank you," she whispered, her voice breaking with emotion. "Thank you for bringing me through the fire to this moment."

She had survived Cordelia's cruelty, lived through years on the streets, endured hunger and cold and the constant fear of discovery. She had protected the children who found their way to her, built a community from nothing, and somehow emerged with her faith intact. Her parents' lessons about resilience and hope had carried her through every trial, just as her mother had promised they would.

The months that followed passed in a blur of restoration and purpose. Holly threw herself into reclaiming Roseworth with the same determination that had once helped her survive on Ashford's streets. The cottage needed extensive repairs—the roof leaked, several windows were broken, and damp had crept into the walls—but each improvement felt like an act of love rather than mere necessity.

Her first decision surprised no one who knew her heart. She hired workers from among the street poor, offering honest employment to those society had forgotten. Nell arrived on the second day, her eyes bright with excitement as she surveyed the cottage.

"Look at this place, Holly," Nell said, running her hand along the kitchen's stone walls. "It's got good bones, this house. We'll make it sing again."

Benjamin came the following week, his basket-weaving skills proving invaluable for storage solutions and his steady temperament helping organise the renovation work. He appointed himself supervisor of the garden restoration, approaching the wilderness of roses with the same methodical patience he brought to all his tasks.

"Your mother knew what she was about," he told Holly one afternoon as they worked side by side, carefully pruning back the most aggressive climbers. "These roses have been taking care of themselves all this time. They just need a bit of guidance to remember their proper places."

Holly transformed the cottage into a school for destitute children, knocking down walls to create airy classrooms and installing large windows that filled the spaces with light. She purchased slate boards, primers, and maps, recreating the learning environment she'd dreamed of during those cold nights under Ashford's bridges.

The children began arriving before the school was officially ready. Word spread through the city's poorest quarters that Holly Clarke had returned to Roseworth, and the desperate found their way to her door just as they always had. She welcomed them all—the frightened, the hungry, the forgotten ones who reminded her of her own darkest days.

Eight-year-old Maisie was among the first, clutching her younger brother's hand as they stood uncertainly in the cottage's doorway. Holly knelt to their level, remembering how Daniel had once offered his handkerchief to comfort her scraped knee.

"Would you like to learn to read?" she asked gently. "We have books here, and plenty of room for everyone."

The children nodded eagerly, and Holly felt her heart expand with familiar purpose. This was what her mother's roses had been teaching her all along—that beauty could flourish even in the harshest conditions, that love planted in darkness could bloom into something magnificent.

Each evening, Holly walked through the restored garden, watching the sunset paint the cottage walls with golden light. The roses were learning their new boundaries, responding to careful tending with spectacular displays of colour and fragrance. Inside, children's voices echoed through rooms that had stood silent for too long, filling the empty spaces with laughter and hope.

She had come home at last, carrying with her everything she'd learned about survival and faith and the transformative power of love. The cottage breathed with new life, just as her heart had learned to bloom again.

AMONG THE ROSES

S pring arrived at Roseworth like a miracle. After months of careful tending, the rose gardens erupted in a symphony of colour that took Holly's breath away each morning. Pink damask roses cascaded over the stone walls in perfumed waterfalls, whilst deep crimson climbers wound their way up the cottage's grey walls like nature's own tapestry. White roses, pure as her mother's wedding dress, clustered around the kitchen window, and sunny yellow blooms nodded cheerfully beside the front gate.

Holly stood amongst them on a warm May evening, her fingers trailing over the soft petals of a particularly magnificent pink specimen. The air hung heavy with fragrance, and bees hummed contentedly as they moved from bloom to bloom. She closed her eyes and breathed deeply, remembering her mother's hands guiding hers amongst these very bushes all those years ago.

"Even in ashes, they bloom again," she whispered, her mother's final words echoing in the garden's peace.

The roses had survived seven years of neglect, enduring harsh winters and choking weeds, yet here they stood in triumphant splendour. They had grown wild and magnificent, their beauty enhanced rather than diminished by their struggles. Holly saw herself reflected in their resilience—a girl who had lost everything, lived rough on the streets, faced death and betrayal, yet somehow emerged with her capacity for love intact.

Inside the cottage, she could hear the children preparing for evening prayers. Twenty of them lived at Roseworth now, ranging from five-year-old Timothy to fifteen-year-old Margaret, who helped teach the younger ones their letters. Their voices drifted through the open windows, mixing with the garden's evening chorus of birdsong and rustling leaves.

Holly wore a simple blue dress—not her mended one from the streets, but a new gown Daniel had insisted on purchasing when she protested she had no need for finery. The fabric moved softly against her skin as she walked deeper into the garden, following the familiar paths her mother had once tended with such devotion.

She paused beside the largest rose bush, a magnificent damask whose branches stretched nearly to the cottage's second storey. This had been her mother's favourite, the one they'd always tended together. Holly reached out to touch a particularly perfect bloom, its petals soft as silk beneath her fingertips.

"Holly."

She turned at the sound of her name, her heart lifting as it always did when she heard Daniel's voice. He stood at the garden's edge, still dressed in his barrister's robes from a day spent in court. The evening light caught the gentle intelligence in his dark eyes and highlighted the strong line of his jaw.

He had been wonderfully patient these past months, visiting daily but never pressing, allowing her the time she needed to feel truly safe in her new life. He brought books for the children, helped with legal matters regarding the school, and listened with genuine interest as she shared her dreams for

Roseworth's future. Yet Holly had sensed something building between them, a tension that spoke of words unspoken and feelings carefully held in check.

Daniel walked toward her through the roses, his expression serious yet tender. When he reached her, he took her hands in his, his thumbs stroking gently over her knuckles.

"Holly," he began, his voice thick with emotion. "I have loved you since we were young, running around and climbing trees in this very garden. I loved you when you were a flower seller in rags, and I love you now, standing in your mother's garden. I will love you all my days."

Holly's breath caught as Daniel released her hands and dropped to one knee amongst the roses. The fading sunlight created a golden halo around his dark hair, and his eyes never left hers as he spoke.

"You once said we come from different worlds. But we don't —we both come from the same place, the place your father showed me: a world where faith matters more than fortune, where character outweighs class, where love is the greatest gift. Holly Clarke, would you do me the immeasurable honour of becoming my wife?"

For a heartbeat, Holly simply stared at him, overwhelmed by the rightness of this moment. Here, surrounded by her mother's roses in full bloom, with the cottage filled with children's laughter and hope restored to every corner of her world, Daniel knelt before her offering his heart.

Joy bubbled up from deep within her chest, spilling over in a laugh that was half sob. She reached down and grasped his hands, pulling him to his feet with surprising strength.

"Yes, Daniel Thornhill," she said, her voice breaking with happiness. "Yes, with all my heart."

She threw her arms around his neck and kissed him, tasting tears she hadn't realised were falling. Daniel's arms encircled her waist, lifting her slightly off the ground as he spun her amongst the roses, both of them laughing and crying at once.

When they finally broke apart, Holly kept her hands on his shoulders, studying his beloved face in the twilight. "I love you," she whispered, the words feeling like a prayer. "I think I've loved you since you offered me your handkerchief when we were children."

Daniel cupped her face in his hands, his thumbs brushing away her tears. Around them, the roses seemed to nod their approval in the gentle evening breeze, their perfume blessing this moment with sweetness and promise.

DEVOTION

*H*olly stood before the mirror, her reflection wavering through tears she refused to let fall. The ivory silk gown had belonged to Daniel's grandmother, carefully altered to fit Holly's slender frame.

"You look beautiful, dear one." Nell's voice came from behind her, warm with affection. Her dearest friend had traded her patchwork street clothes for a simple yellow dress—a gift from Daniel's mother, who had insisted that Holly's closest companions be properly attired for the wedding.

Holly touched her cheek, looking at her reflection. "Mother would have loved this day."

"She sees it," Nell said firmly, fastening the tiny buttons at Holly's wrists. "Both your parents see it, and they're proud."

Benjamin appeared in the doorway, his new clothes pressed and his hair neatly combed. In his arms he carried the bridal bouquet—roses from every bush in the garden, their colours ranging from deepest crimson to palest blush. White damask roses, her mother's favourites, formed the heart of the arrangement.

"The carriage is ready," he announced, though his voice

cracked slightly on the words. "Half of Ashford Green's already at the church."

Holly lifted the bouquet to her face, breathing in the familiar perfume that had sustained her through the darkest years. The roses had bloomed magnificently this spring, as if celebrating their return to beloved hands.

The rebuilt church of St Nicholas rose before them, its new stone gleaming golden in the afternoon sun. Holly's breath caught as she stepped from the carriage and saw the crowd gathered outside—not just the expected gentry and professional classes, but faces she recognised from the streets and markets. Mrs Patterson stood beside Lady Pemberton. Tom and Sarah from the flower stalls chatted easily with Cambridge barristers. The children from her school pressed against the church railings, their faces scrubbed clean and eyes bright with excitement.

Sir Richard waited at the church entrance, distinguished in his formal attire. When he saw Holly, his weathered face softened with genuine emotion.

"Miss Clarke," he said, offering his arm. "This is the greatest privilege of my life."

Holly placed her hand on his sleeve, drawing strength from his steady presence. "Thank you for everything, Sir Richard. For believing in me, for protecting me."

"Your father would be immensely proud," he replied quietly. "As am I."

The church doors opened, and the congregation rose as one. Holly's eyes found Daniel immediately—he stood at the altar in his finest black coat, his face radiant with joy. Beside him waited the new rector, a kind man who had heard their story and insisted on performing the ceremony himself.

As they proceeded down the aisle, Holly marvelled at the extraordinary gathering. Little Jim from the streets sat between a magistrate and his wife, all three sharing a hymnal. Gracie and the other children occupied an entire pew, their faces glowing with pride. Former street dwellers sat beside county families, united in witness to this moment.

Daniel's eyes never left hers as Sir Richard placed her hand in his. The familiar calluses on Daniel's palm spoke of honest work and gentle strength. When the rector asked who gave this woman in marriage, Sir Richard's voice rang clear: "Her family does—all of us."

The service began, and Holly felt her parents' presence as surely as if they stood beside her. When Daniel spoke his vows, his words carried across the hushed congregation like a prayer made manifest.

"Holly, you have shown me that God brings beauty from ashes, that faith rewards those who endure, and that love triumphs over every darkness. I promise to stand beside you as we tend the garden we will plant together."

Holly's voice trembled as she began her own vows, the words she had whispered to the roses during countless evenings of preparation.

"Daniel, you found me when I was lost and loved me when I had nothing to offer but a broken heart. You saw worth where others saw only a beggar girl. Through you, God showed me that roses truly do bloom again, even from the deepest ashes."

Her voice grew stronger, carrying across the packed church. "I promise to walk beside you in faith, to tend the garden of our love with the same devotion my mother taught me, and to remember always that our greatest treasures are not gold or land, but the souls we serve together."

The rector smiled as Daniel slipped his grandmother's gold band onto Holly's finger. "By the power vested in me, I now pronounce you husband and wife. Daniel, you may kiss your bride."

Daniel's hands cupped her face with infinite tenderness before his lips met hers. The congregation erupted in joyous applause—children cheering, women weeping, men calling out blessings. Flower petals rained down as they turned to face their extraordinary gathering, this unlikely family bound not by blood but by love.

Holly clutched her roses and Daniel's hand as they walked back down the aisle, her heart finally, completely whole.

FULL CIRCLE

$\mathcal{H}$olly stood at the window of Thornhill Manor's morning room, watching Daniel cross the courtyard with their three children trailing behind him like eager ducklings. At eight, Thomas had his father's serious expression but his mother's gentle heart. Six-year-old Mary possessed her grandmother's auburn curls and an irrepressible curiosity about everything that grew. Little James, barely four, clutched a wooden horse in one pudgy fist whilst attempting to keep pace with his siblings.

"Mama, Papa says we can visit the school today," Thomas announced as they tumbled through the French doors, bringing the scent of roses and morning sunshine.

"After we tend the garden," Holly replied, smoothing Mary's windswept hair. "The roses need deadheading."

The arrangement had worked beautifully these past seven years. Thornhill Manor provided the children stability and proper education, whilst Roseworth remained Holly's heart—the school and refuge that had grown from seventeen street children into a county-wide network of hope. Three dozen children now lived permanently at the cottage, with Nell managing the domestic arrangements and Benjamin overseeing the gardens and workshops where older children learned trades.

"Tell us the story, Mama," Mary pleaded, settling cross-legged on the Turkish carpet. "About the little girl and the roses."

Holly exchanged an amused glance with Daniel, who had heard this request countless times. Their children never tired of hearing how their parents met, though Holly carefully edited the darker chapters for young ears.

"Very well," Holly said, gathering James onto her lap whilst Thomas and Mary leaned closer. "Once upon a time, there was a little girl who lived in a cottage surrounded by the most beautiful roses in all the world."

"Like the roses at the cottage?" James interrupted, his thumb finding its way to his mouth.

"Exactly like those, darling. Those very same roses, planted by her grandmother's grandmother." Holly's voice took on the cadence of beloved repetition. "The little girl's mama taught her that roses were very special flowers, because even when terrible things happened—even when winter came and everything looked dead—if you tended them with love and patience, they would always bloom again."

Thomas frowned thoughtfully. "But what terrible things happened?"

Holly chose her words carefully. "The little girl lost her mama and papa when she was very young. She had to go live with people who weren't kind to her, and for a while, she forgot about the roses. She lived in a place where everything seemed grey and hopeless."

"But she remembered!" Mary exclaimed, having heard this part before.

"She did remember. And do you know what helped her?"

Holly looked at each child in turn. "Other children who needed hope, just like she did. She discovered that when you share your bread with hungry people, when you teach letters to children who can't read, when you tell stories about faith to those who have forgotten how to believe—well, that's how you tend the garden of your heart."

Daniel settled into his chair, his eyes soft with the memory of first seeing Holly amongst her street children.

"And then," Holly continued, "God sent someone very special to help her remember that she was loved, that she had worth, and that the roses had been waiting for her all along."

"Papa!" the children chorused.

"Your papa saw past her patched dress and dirty hands. He saw her heart." Holly reached for Daniel's hand. "And together, they came back to the cottage and discovered something wonderful."

"What?" James whispered.

"The roses had grown wild and strong whilst she was gone. They covered every wall, every fence, every corner of the garden. They had been waiting faithfully, just as God's love waits faithfully for us." Holly's voice thickened with emotion. "And now they bloom more beautifully than ever before, because they shelter and feed so many others."

Thomas studied the view seriously. "So the story is about never giving up?"

"It's about remembering that even in the darkest winter, spring always comes again," Holly replied. "Even when every-thing seems lost, if you keep faith and tend to others with love, beautiful things will grow."

Mary tugged at Holly's skirt. "Mama, will our roses always bloom?"

Holly knelt beside her daughter, seeing her own green eyes reflected in the child's face. "Always, my darling. As long as there are hands to tend them and hearts to remember their story."

Daniel joined them, gathering his family close as they watched their legacy unfold below—children laughing, learning, growing strong in the garden where love had bloomed from ashes, exactly as it was meant to be.

THE FIRST CHAPTER OF 'THE ORPHAN'S WORKHOUSE TRIAL'

The sun's gentle rays danced through the curtained window of the Whitmore parsonage, casting golden patterns across Catherine's bedroom. Her small collection of cloth dolls and wooden animals seemed to come alive in the morning light, shadows playing across the spines of cherished books that lined her modest shelf.

Catherine stirred beneath her blankets, her bright blue eyes fluttering open. For a moment, she simply lay there, listening to the melodious chirping of sparrows that had made their nest in the oak tree outside. A smile spread across her face as she stretched her arms above her head, wiggling her toes beneath the warm covers.

"Catherine? Are you awake, dear one?" Her mother's melodic voice floated up the narrow staircase.

"Yes, Mother!" Catherine called back, throwing off her blankets with sudden enthusiasm.

She padded across the wooden floorboards to her small dresser, selecting a simple frock in robin egg blue—her favourite colour. The fabric was soft from many washings but still bore the careful stitching her mother had added along the hem last spring. Catherine dressed quickly, humming a hymn they'd sung in church the previous Sunday.

Standing before the small oval mirror mounted on her wall, Catherine wove her chestnut brown hair into a neat braid, her nimble fingers working with practiced efficiency. A few wayward strands escaped, framing her heart-shaped face. She tucked them behind her ears, studying her reflection with a critical eye before nodding with satisfaction.

"Catherine! The morning waits for no one," her mother called again, amusement evident in her tone.

Catherine flew down the stairs, nearly colliding with her father who was emerging from his study, a leather-bound Bible tucked under his arm.

"Careful there, my little whirlwind," he chuckled, steadying her with a gentle hand.

"Sorry, Father! Mother and I have gardening to do!"

Without pausing for breakfast, Catherine darted through the kitchen and flung open the back door. The cool morning air greeted her, along with the scent of damp earth and blooming flowers. She kicked off her shoes at the doorstep, sighing with delight as her bare feet sank into the dewy grass.

"There you are," Mary Whitmore looked up from where she knelt beside a patch of herbs, a smile warming her gentle features. The morning light caught the auburn highlights in her hair, pulled back in a practical bun. "I was beginning to think you might sleep the day away."

"Never!" Catherine declared, skipping toward the flower beds that bordered their modest garden. "The flowers would miss me too much."

Her mother laughed, the sound like wind chimes in a summer breeze. "Indeed they would."

Catherine wandered among the colourful blooms, carefully selecting the brightest specimens. The garden behind the parsonage was Mary's pride—a patchwork of medicinal herbs, vegetables for their table, and flowers that brightened both their home and the church altar.

"Look, Mother!" Catherine exclaimed, rushing back with her carefully gathered bouquet. "I found the loveliest flowers! Don't the lilacs smell divine?"

Her mother set down her pruning shears and accepted the small bunch, burying her nose in the blossoms. "Absolutely Heavenly. God's handiwork in every petal."

Her mother gently tucked a loose strand of hair behind Catherine's ear. "The rosemary is ready for harvesting. Would you like to learn which herbs are best for easing an aching chest? Mrs. Harris' youngest still has that terrible cough."

Catherine nodded eagerly, following her mother's experienced hands as they moved between the herb beds, the earthy aromas rising around them as they disturbed the leaves.

"This one smells like Christmas," Catherine noted, rubbing a sprig of rosemary between her fingers.

"And works wonders for memory," her mother added, her voice taking on the gentle teaching tone that Catherine loved. "The Romans believed it strengthened the mind."

Together they worked in companionable rhythm, Catherine pulling weeds while her mother pruned and harvested, their conversation flowing easily between plant lore and village news.

Click here to read the rest of
'The Orphan's Workhouse Trial'

Faith. Courage. A Love That Transcends Circumstance.

In the harsh industrial landscape of Victorian Manchester, Catherine Whitmore's world crumbles when cholera claims both her beloved parents. Orphaned and alone, she faces an impossible choice that will test the very foundations of her faith.

Armed with nothing but her unwavering belief in God's plan and the compassionate heart her parents instilled in her, Catherine enters the forbidding walls of O'Brien Workhouse. In a place designed to break spirits, she becomes a beacon of hope for fellow workers drowning in despair.

When unexpected attention from those in power offers her a glimpse of an easier life, Catherine must navigate treacherous waters of privilege and hidden motives. But it's in the most unlikely places that she discovers true friendship—and perhaps something deeper—with someone who shares her faith and dreams of a better world.

As Catherine's compassionate spirit begins to touch hearts throughout the workhouse, not everyone welcomes the changes she inspires. When crisis strikes, Catherine must choose between personal safety and standing firm in her convictions.

Can faith triumph over adversity? Will love find a way across the rigid boundaries of Victorian society? And can one young woman's courage transform not just her own destiny, but the lives of all those around her?
From the peaceful parsonage of her childhood to the industrial heart of Manchester, Catherine's journey weaves together threads of loss, faith, and the transformative power of compassion. In a world that measures worth by wealth, can the true riches of character finally shine through?

'The Orphan's Workhouse Trial'

OUR GIFT TO YOU

AS A WAY TO SAY THANK YOU WE WOULD LOVE TO SEND YOU THIS BEAUTIFUL STORY FREE OF CHARGE.

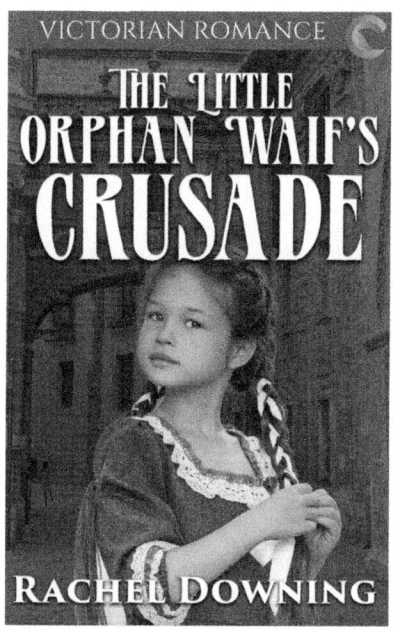

Click here for your FREE COPY of

'The Little Orphan Waif's Crusade'

CornerstoneTales.com/sign-up

In the wake of her father's passing, seven-year-old Matilda is determined to heal her sister Effie's shattered spirit.

Desperate to restore joy to Effie's life, Matilda embarks on a daring quest, aided by the gentle-hearted postman, Philip. Together, they weave a plan to ignite the flame of love in Effie's heart once more.

At Cornerstone Tales we publish books you can trust. Great tales without sex or swearing, but with all of the mystery and romance you expect from a great story.

Be the first to know when we release new books, take part in our fun competitions, and get surprise free books in your inbox by signing up to our free VIP Reader list.

As a thank you you'll receive a copy of 'The Little Orphan Waif's Crusade' straight away, alongside other gifts.

Click here to sign up for our mailing list, and receive your FREE stories.

CornerstoneTales.com/sign-up

LOVE VICTORIAN ROMANCE?

Other Rachel Downing Books

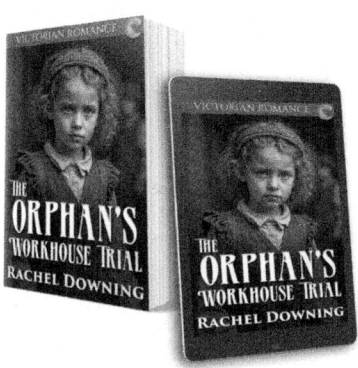

The Orphan's Workhouse Trial

In the harsh industrial landscape of Victorian Manchester, Catherine Whitmore's world crumbles when cholera claims both her beloved parents. Orphaned and alone, she faces an impossible choice that will test the very foundations of her faith.

Get 'The Orphan's Workhouse Trial' Here!

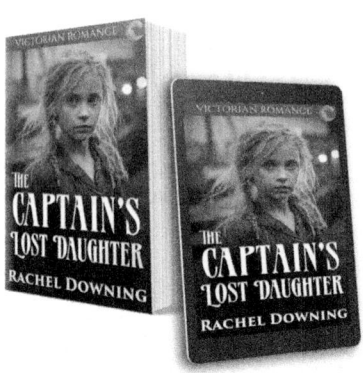

The Captain's Lost Daughter

In 1847, eight-year-old Evangeline's world is torn apart when a violent shipwreck separates her from her beloved father, Captain Thomas Hartwell. Cast adrift and alone, Eva must find the strength to survive in a world that shows no mercy to orphaned children.

Get 'The Captain's Lost Daughter' Here!

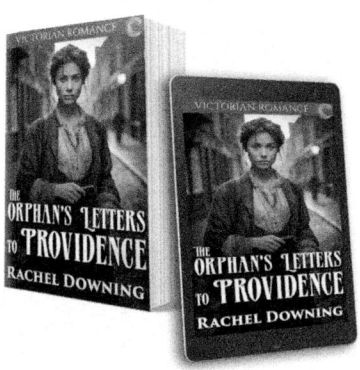

The Orphan's Letters to Providence

In the windswept Yorkshire countryside, Alice Wells's world shatters when tragedy strikes her beloved parents. Orphaned and thrust into a hostile household, she clings to his dying words: "Write to Providence, dear heart."

Get 'The Orphan's Letters to Providence' Here!

The Forsaken Lacemaker of Hampstead

In the shadow of Victorian London, Mabel Fairchild's life is shattered by false accusations and devastating loss. With two younger siblings dependent on her care, she makes an impossible promise: to keep her family together despite the world's cruel intentions.

Get 'The Forsaken Lacemaker of Hampstead' Here!

The Workhouse Orphan's Redemption

In the brutal world of Victorian London, Emma Redbrook's life begins in tragedy. Orphaned and trapped in Grimshaw's Workhouse, she endures cruelty that would break most spirits. But Emma's unwavering faith becomes her beacon of hope — and her strength.

Get 'The Workhouse Orphan's Redemption' Here!

The Orphan's Christmas Hymn

Seven-year-old Clara Winters' world shatters when tragedy strikes days before Christmas. Sent to St. Mary's Church Orphanage, she finds her only solace in the hymns that once filled her happy home. When her angelic voice catches the attention of the kind-hearted Reverend Thornton and his musically gifted son Edward, Clara dares to dream of a brighter future.

Get 'The Orphan's Christmas Hymn' Here!

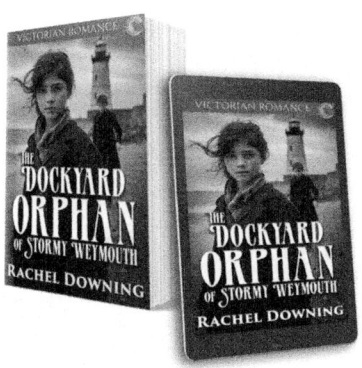

The Dockyard Orphan of Stormy Weymouth

Sarah Campbell's world crumbles when a tragic accident claims her parents' lives. She finds solace in the lighthouse's beam that guides ships to safety. But it's a young fisherman wrestling with his own loss, who truly captures her heart.

Get 'The Dockyard Orphan of Stormy Weymouth' Here!

The Workhouse Orphan Rivals

Childhood sweethearts torn apart. A promise broken. A love that refuses to die.

Get 'The Workhouse Orphan Rivals' Here!

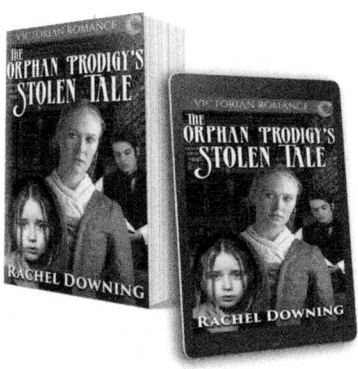

The Orphan Prodigy's Stolen Tale

When ten-year-old Isabella Farmerson's world shatters with the tragic loss of her parents, she's thrust into a life of hardship and uncertainty.

Get 'The Orphan Prodigy's Stolen Tale' Here!

The Lost Orphans of Dark Streets

Follow the stories of Elizabeth and Molly as they negotiate the dangerous slums and find their place in the world.

Get 'The Lost Orphans of Dark Streets' Here!

Two Steadfast Orphan's Dreams

Follow the stories of Isabella and Ada as they overcome all odds and find love.

Get 'Two Steadfast Orphan's Dreams' Here!

And from our other Victorian Romance Author Dorothy Wellings...

The Moral Maid's Unjust Trial

Matilda must fend for herself when her father is wrongfully accused for a crime he didn't commit.

Get 'The Moral Maid's Unjust Trial' Here!

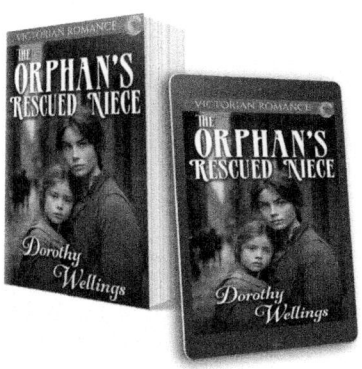

The Orphan's Rescued Niece

As Beatrice grows from a wide-eyed child into a resilient young woman, she finds herself caught between her love for her troubled brother and her desire for a life free from poverty and fear.

Get 'The Orphan's Rescued Niece' Here!

The Lost Orphan of the Parish

Annabelle's world shatters when illness claims her beloved parents. Left alone at ten years old with no inheritance, she's sent to the harsh Thornfield Orphanage with nothing but her father's worn Bible and the memories of his gentle teachings.

Get 'The Lost Orphan of the Parish' Here!

The Orphan Angel's Grace

Grace's world is illuminated by her father's love and the warm glow of London's gas lamps he tends each night. Living humbly but happily above a Whitechapel bakery, ten-year-old Grace treasures her father's stories of her saintly mother and learns the healing arts from her mother's cherished prayer book.

Get 'The Orphan Angel's Grace' Here!

The Lost Orphan's Found Family

Ten-year-old Annabelle's world is confined to the stern walls of St Catherine's Orphanage, yet her spirit shines bright as London's gas lamps. Despite the harsh conditions and limited resources, Belle finds joy in tending the orphanage garden, caring for younger children, and reading worn Bible stories by candlelight, her unshakeable faith illuminating even the darkest moments.

Get 'The Lost Orphan's Found Family' Here!

The Steadfast Seamstress of Seven Dials

When harsh winter takes her mother's life, Mercy Whitfield finds herself alone in the unforgiving streets of London's Seven Dials. Armed only with her mother's precious sewing box, a small Bible, and extraordinary skill with needle and thread, she must navigate a world that shows little mercy to orphaned girls.

Get 'The Steadfast Seamstress of Seven Dials' Here!

If you enjoyed this story, sign up to our mailing list to be the first to hear about our new releases and any sales and deals we have.

We also want to offer you a Victorian Romance novella - 'The Little Orphan Waif's Crusade' - absolutely free!

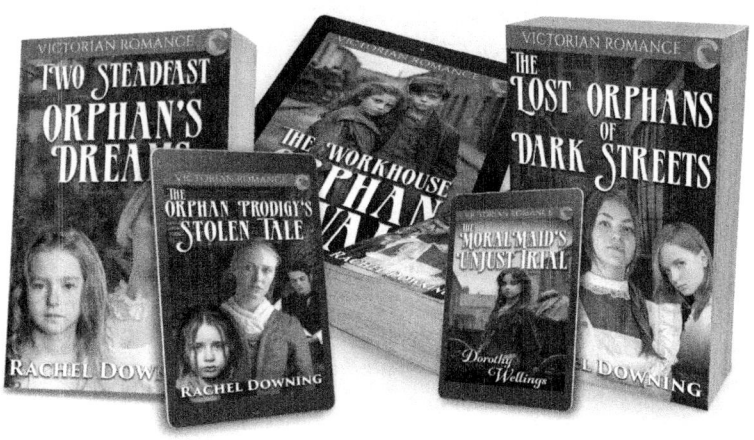

Click here to sign up for our mailing list, and receive your FREE stories.

CornerstoneTales.com/sign-up

Printed in Dunstable, United Kingdom